TO FIND A WITCH

TO FIND A WITCH

THE WITCH NEXT DOOR™ BOOK FIVE

JUDITH BERENS

LMBPN Publishing
PMB 196, 2540 South Maryland Pkwy
Las Vegas, NV 89109

First US edition, October 2019
ebook ISBN: 978-1-64202-513-2
Print ISBN: 978-1-64202-514-9

THE TO FIND A WITCH TEAM

Thanks to the JIT Readers

Dave Hicks
Jeff Eaton
Peter Manis
Deb Mader
Larry Omans
Jeff Goode

If we've missed anyone, please let us know!

Editor
SkyHunter Editing Team

DEDICATIONS

From Martha

To everyone who still believes in magic
and all the possibilities that holds.
To all the readers who make this
entire ride so much fun.
And to my son, Louie and so many wonderful friends who
remind me all the time of what
really matters and how wonderful
life can be in any given moment.

From Michael

To Family, Friends and
Those Who Love
To Read.
May We All Enjoy Grace
To Live The Life We Are
Called.

ONE

"Come on, Lil." Seated on a large, flat rock on the beach, Romeo Stephens tilted his head, the gesture a little impatient, and fixed her with a firm look. "You've been at this for almost four hours without a break."

Lily Antony raised her hands toward the waves of the Black Sea on the eastern coast of Romania and shook her head. "I've almost got it," she muttered in protest.

"How will you know when you've mastered this spell? You don't really even know what it is—"

"I will, okay?" She took a deep breath and clapped sharply. This time, though, she held her palms together for a few seconds longer than she had in all her previous attempts in the last four hours.

"Lily..." He pushed himself up from the rock to stand barefoot in the sand. "It's probably a good idea to take a break. Call it for the day."

She glanced briefly at him and turned her attention to her hands once more. Beyond them, the ocean and the open sky stretched out farther than she could see. "I need to learn this."

He stepped slowly toward her. "You need to sleep—"

"Romeo, I got this!" She gritted her teeth and summoned the same black cloud she'd pulled up between her hands all evening. Her arms trembled as she drew her palms farther and farther apart. The thick, roiling, crackling mass of her most powerful spell churned in the space between them. Thick streaks of silver light flashed within the magical darkness and reflected in her glassy, exhausted eyes.

With a soft sigh, he stopped only a few yards away and watched, his expression one of concern.

When she felt she could no longer sustain the black cloud as it was, she had two options—drop it completely until it fizzled into useless nothingness, or send it out. *If this is what you do, Mom, I can do it too. I won't give up.*

The pressure built inside her chest and behind her eyes until she could no longer contain it. With a shout, she flung her arms out to the sides and willed the spell she didn't yet understand to do what it was meant to do.

The black cloud erupted with a flash of light, and a massive shadow-bird that smelled like ash and smoke and power lurched from her chest and the shadowed mass between her hands at the same time. The creature uttered its own cry—a warning shriek that might have been defiance—and soared over the choppy waters of the sea until it vanished against the darkened horizon.

Inside the 2002 Winnebago Adventurer behind them —which they'd driven across North America, South America, and now Europe—the silver heron coin on the shelf above her side of the bed rattled and darkened with a dense black shadow. In the next moment, it fell still.

By the time she could no longer see the last fluttering wisps of her magic's black smoke, she was on her knees in the sand, breathing heavily. Romeo had already dropped beside her.

"Lily?" He put a gentle hand on her back. "Are you okay?"

She sighed, felt the softness of the beach beneath the backs of her hands, and turned her head to look at him with a smirk. "Well, that was something, wasn't it?"

He huffed a wary laugh and stared in the direction of wherever her shadow-bird had gone. "Yeah. That was definitely something. Now you're done for tonight, right?"

"No." Lily swallowed and set one foot on the sand so she could push herself up. "That was a step in the right direction, for sure. But I can't stop until I work out how that spells operates and how it'll open the—"

"Woah." He caught her when she swayed sideways and almost tripped over him. While he steadied her, he scrambled to his feet and couldn't help but frown. "You can stop. You have to. This is wearing you out, and I'm not exactly sure how safe it is to keep going like this when you can barely stand. Plus, it's almost completely dark. So... how bout dinner and sleep?"

Her hand grasped his forearm as tightly as she could— a definite sign of her current weakness—and she sighed and looked out at the dark water. "Yeah. Yeah, okay. At least I made some progress."

"Right. Considerable progress." He removed her fingers' death grip on his forearm gently and held her hand instead. "You'll find out what everything means and how to make it all work for you, Lil. You always do. But it's really not gonna mean anything if you hurt yourself in the process. There is nothing wrong with slowing down and taking a little more time for yourself."

Romeo led her across the sand toward the Winnie. "For food. And sleep. And...life. You know, like a normal person."

She snorted, and although she smiled at him, he knew he hadn't convinced her completely. "I'm not a normal person, Romeo. I'm not even a normal witch."

"Yep." He sighed, and his smile faded a little. "I've always known that about you."

"But you didn't really know how not normal I actually am." She shrugged and walked closely at his side, her legs and arms still shaking slightly. "Honestly, I'm only starting to realize that myself."

"Or maybe you're only starting to realize that you can't ignore how kickass you are."

For the first time that day, she finally laughed. "I've never had a doubt about that."

He smirked. "Okay. You can't downplay it anymore. How 'bout that?" He opened the Winnebago's side door and held it for her.

Lily steadied herself against the frame to take the first high step inside, caught the edge of the kitchen counter, and pulled herself up the other two steps. "So you're saying I've seriously underestimated myself. Is that it?"

"Well, yeah, but I'm not the first to say that. I think that's what everyone's tried to tell you since we left Charleston." The door closed behind him, and he placed a hand on her lower back before he stepped around her into the RV's tiny kitchen. "It's what your mom tried to tell you for...jeez. Forever, probably."

"Yeah..." She crossed the small space on shaky legs and lowered herself into the booth at the two-person kitchen table. It had become automatic, now, to slide her legs around the large red pot of perpetually growing wolfsbane the nine-year-old witch Rosalía had given them in Mexico. "I only wish she could've told me more about what that black-cloud spell is supposed to be. Or do. All I really have is my vision in the Ochiului crypt, and that showed me enough to know it's important."

Romeo shuddered before he opened the fridge. "Don't call it a crypt."

"Why not?"

"It makes it sound creepier than it already is."

She grinned at him. "Well, what else would you prefer?"

"Well, sepulcher doesn't sound half as bad."

Her chuckle revealed her weariness. "You know that's basically the same thing, right?"

He shrugged and studied the contents of the fridge. "I guess. But it sounds a little like okra, and right now, I could really go for some of Janice Garber's pickled okra."

"What are you talking about?"

His grin was intended to tease a small laugh from her. It had been a long day of not once hearing that sound.

"She's married to one of my dad's friends. The woman pickles and jars almost everything, and I'm tellin' ya, there's no one in the South who can pickle okra like Janice. Or fry it. Mmm." He shook his head and retrieved the container with the leftover polenta dish from the day before. "I never thought I'd say it, but I'm starting to miss Southern cooking."

"You're gonna make something else, too, right?"

"Are you that hungry?" He set a pan on the stove and turned the burner on.

"No, I'd say I'm at normal hunger levels. But that's not enough for both of us."

He turned toward her, and another frown settled between his eyebrows. "I already ate."

"When?"

"About two hours ago. When I asked if you wanted to stop for dinner, and you simply... Well, you didn't hear me, I guess."

"Oh." Lily leaned back in the booth and stared at the table. "You don't have to make me dinner now if I already missed it."

"I know." He stirred the polenta and shrugged casually. "I want to."

"Well...thanks."

A few minutes later, he slid the food onto a plate and brought it to her with a fork and a bottle of water. "So that was your first shadow-bird, huh?"

She smiled at him as he set the plate in front of her and wiggled into the booth that was still too low for his long legs to fit comfortably. "Yeah. The first one ever. Are you okay?"

He grimaced and shifted again. "Yeah, it's only this—"

"Ow." She winced as his foot connected with her shin.

"Oh. Sorry." He shot her a sheepish smile and scoffed. "We need to find a better place for that pot."

"Or we could simply do what Melissa did and hang the wolfsbane from the ceiling." She glanced up. "In a different pot, I mean."

"It's kinda the lowest thing on the priority list right now." He set his elbow on the table and propped his chin up with both hands. "You need to eat something."

"And you asked me about the shadow-bird."

"I'm simply making friendly conversation."

Lily snorted. "Okay." She took a mouthful of steaming polenta and sausage and washed it down with a long drink of water. "So, yeah. That was my first shadow-bird. It looked like my mom's, didn't it?" He nodded and gave her food a pointed glance, so she took another forkful. "The vision I had in that...chamber..."

"Better."

"Okay, we'll go with that." She shook her head with a small smile. "It showed me that the black cloud and the shadow-bird are both important to activate the heron coin. It merely didn't show me how."

"Huh." Romeo pursed his lips. "It was kind of a useless vision, then."

"Well, I don't think very many visions from a giant floating eye made of blue fire come with step-by-step instructions." She raised an eyebrow.

"Bummer."

She took another mouthful and chewed thoughtfully for a while.

"I know you don't really want me to find the answers."

"What?" He sat upright in the booth. "That's not true." All it took was for her to stare at him in a silent challenge and he knew he had to continue. "I definitely want you to work it out. That's how we find your mom, right?"

"Right. But—"

"But I really don't like that coin, Lil. I don't like that you're wearing yourself out trying to activate it. And I really don't like the fact that when you do, the Black Heron's gonna know exactly where you are. Even that old Romani witch thought they'd use it to target you next."

Lily narrowed her eyes at him. "You really don't like her, do you?"

For a few seconds, he didn't say anything. "Not really, no. Whatever kind of power she had over werewolves... Yeah, I wasn't too fond of being told to sit and heel while you were down in that secret chamber by yourself. And I really didn't like the fact that she didn't even try to convince you to not use that coin. I don't think she cares about what happens to you, honestly."

"She was only protecting her people, Romeo."

"Yeah, I get that. But she didn't try to protect you at all."

"Maybe that's because I don't need to be protected." She continued to stare at him, her fork poised over the plate.

He wanted to argue with that but he'd learned a long time ago that it was a bad idea to argue with Lily Antony, especially when it came down to what she could and couldn't do on her own. "I know." He sighed. "Yeah, I know that. But it doesn't mean I have to like it."

Lily ate a few more mouthfuls and drank more water. "Do you want the rest of this? I'm...not that hungry, I guess."

"Seriously?"

"A hundred percent. I ate, what? Half of it. I'll probably be hungry again in the morning."

"Sure." Without asking whether he agreed to her allegedly renewed appetite after sleep or to eat the rest of her dinner, she pushed the plate across the tiny table toward him. He wolfed down what remained in four heaped forkfuls, maneuvered his legs around the potted wolfsbane and from under the table with as much difficulty as before, and stood. "I'll clean up. Why don't you get a head start on that sleep?" He headed toward the sink.

"Romeo?" She gave him a reassuring smile when he turned to look at her. "Thank you."

He nodded. "You know I have your back, Lil. And you're welcome."

While he washed the plate, she pushed out of the booth and walked down the short, narrow hallway toward the bedroom at the back of the Winnie. *Maybe I did push myself a little too hard. I feel like I haven't slept in days.* She crawled onto the foot of the queen-sized mattress and made her way toward the headboard. When she rose on her knees to pull the comforter back, a glint of silver from the shelf above the bed caught her eye.

Right beside her wooden box with the lily flower

carved into the lid—which was now completely empty but had once held the stone head that had led them to Ichacál —was the silver coin with the heron etched onto its surface. The sigil of the Black Heron Society and the crazed magicals holding Greta Antony captive seemed innocuous, a mere decoration, but she knew better. "I'll find out what I need to know, Mom," she whispered and stared at the coin. "I promise. And then I'll come to get you—"

A shadow moved across the surface of the coin and she froze for a moment. *I guess I'm hallucinating too.*

Romeo turned the faucet off in the kitchen. "So...the light's still on. I assume that means you're not actually asleep."

Lily pried herself away from the coin, turned, and slipped under the covers fully clothed as he appeared in the doorway. "It's not an instant process, you know."

"Funny. It is for me."

She grinned and patted the empty place on the bed beside her. "Then get over here and go to sleep already. It might make it easier for me."

With a little chuckle, he turned the small bedroom light off and moved to the bed. "That's actually kinda sweet."

"What's sweet?" She watched his silhouette climb onto the bed before he slid under the covers and drew her to him.

"You basically told me you can't fall asleep unless I'm right here beside you."

"I don't know... We've spent a couple of months on the road together. That doesn't mean I'm used to it yet."

"Maybe not completely." He pulled her back closer against his chest and placed a light kiss on her neck. "I guess that happens when you stop wearing clothes to bed."

Lily flicked his arm wrapped around her waist and smiled at his soft laughter in her ear. "Keep dreaming, buddy."

"Oh, I will be in about a minute. Night, Lil."

"'Night." Smiling, she closed her eyes but didn't drift off as quickly as he did. She couldn't stop thinking about the black cloud of her most powerful spell, the shadow-bird that matched her mom's, and the silver heron coin that glittered directly above their heads.

TWO

L ily woke the next morning with the sun streaming through the single window in the bedroom. She rolled over and reached instinctively for Romeo, but he wasn't there beside her. As soon as she pushed herself up to lean against the headboard, he appeared in the doorway with two mugs of coffee in hand.

"I had a feeling you'd be up." He smirked and walked toward the back of the bedroom before he sidled along the few feet of space between her side of the bed and the wall. "Do you think you had enough rest?"

She smiled and put her hand out for the coffee he offered her. "What time is it?"

"Almost nine."

"Yeah, that sounds like more than enough rest." With a smile, she lifted the coffee to her lips and took a sip. "This is so good."

"I know." He nodded, took another sip from his cup, and paused. His gaze settled on the recessed shelf above the bed and the silver heron coin that caught the sunlight. "Was that there all night?"

"What?" She set her cup on the nightstand and turned to follow his gaze. "Oh. I meant to put it away. I...uh, didn't think about it."

"That thing gives me the creeps, Lil."

"Yeah, I know." She glanced at him and shrugged. "Sorry."

"It's okay. Can you put it somewhere else, though, please? Literally anywhere but right above our heads when we're sleeping. It's gonna give me nightmares."

She frowned and tried not to laugh. "When was the last time you even had a nightmare?"

"I dunno. A long time. But if I have to sleep under that thing, I'm very sure that's gonna change."

"Okay, okay." She leaned forward to climb onto her knees and turn on the bed. "I'll put it somewhere you won't be able to find it even if you—"

The minute her fingers touched the relic, a blazing light blinded her to everything else—like she'd been caught in the middle of a lightning flash—and she couldn't see a thing. All the breath was sucked out of her lungs, and she tried to shout for Romeo but couldn't speak. She also couldn't move and while she still felt the coin beneath her fingers, the rest of her was...gone.

What the hell is this?

Red lines streaked into the nothingness around her—wherever she was—to cross and intersect like a massive 3D map. Voices intruded into her oddly hollow existence. They were faint at first, as if from really far away, but they grew louder by the second, and closer. Finally, she saw the faces.

One by one, they appeared along the blazing red lines of magic, each figure blue-tinged like smoke. Two men with snakelike eyes leered at her from inside what looked like a tunnel. A warlock with wild, tangled hair—and the telltale, blood-red eyes within an androgynous face—turned from a desk and raised an eyebrow. A group of witches in eveningwear stood in a circle with their arms outstretched in front of an altar. They lowered their hands slowly and tilted their heads as together, they turned to fix her with wide gazes.

She recognized one face within the real-time vignettes of magicals all staring at her. Some whispered, others remained silent in surprise, and a few of them chuckled in dark tones. Someone, although she couldn't be sure who, uttered a screeched cackle. It would have made her jump if she could feel her body. She couldn't turn her attention away from the bald man in the denim jacket, though, whose eyes widened when he saw her in this hidden realm. The pack master's lips twitched into a sneer, and Hugo stepped forward within the small bubble of blue light in which he'd appeared. Behind him, she saw the desert brush of Chihuahua, Mexico, and a line of stunted trees. "There you are." He growled as his eyes flashed silver.

His voice was enough to spur a response from her. Without trying or even knowing how, she jerked her fingers away from the heron coin. Her own raw gasp startled her, and she slumped on her heels and bounced a little on the mattress. The silver coin rattled on the shelf and fell still as if she'd dropped it there, and her breath was pulled out of her again in a rush. The sound of it seemed to finalize the fact that she'd returned to her own body, and her surprise kicked as she scrambled backward across the comforter.

"Lily! What—" Romeo shouted in surprise and pain as fresh, hot coffee spilled down the front of his shorts and his mug clattered to the floor. He sucked in a hissed breath and tried to wipe himself off, but that was useless. "What happened?" He raised a bare foot out of the rapidly cooling puddle on the floor and leaned toward her.

"I did it," she whispered.

"All I saw was you freeze up for a few seconds before you dropped that thing like it was burning you."

Lily glanced at her hand, but that wasn't the problem. "Last night, when I cast that shadow-bird on my own...the raven..."

"You activated the coin."

She looked at him with wide eyes. "I saw the network."

"Are you sure?"

"Hugo was there. The pack master in Mexico—"

"Yeah, I remember." He frowned and obviously didn't enjoy the memory of the werewolf leader who'd kidnapped him, pumped him full of drugs and imbued him with a curse, and chained him to a tree as a contestant for the next wolf fight. "What about your mom?"

"I couldn't..." She clenched her eyes shut and shook her head. "I wasn't ready."

"But you will be. That's how we find her."

"They saw me, Romeo. There are so many magicals

connected to this, and I only had a good look at a few. The rest are..." She swallowed thickly and crawled off the bed. "I need air."

"Do you want me to come with you?"

"Please don't." She'd already stepped through the doorway and into the short hall. "I only need a minute."

By the time he maneuvered around the far side of the bed in an attempt to stop her and make sure she was okay, the Winnie's side door banged shut. He strode into the hall and saw her shoes still on the floor in front of the armchair.

Lily walked along the beach. She didn't particularly care whether anyone saw a young witch suddenly appear from what looked like thin air where she'd conjured an illusion to hide them and the Winnebago. It was a good idea to conceal one RV and two foreign magicals on an otherwise empty beach but now, it made her feel lost. A few jagged stones bit into her feet. She couldn't focus on stepping carefully and she barely felt the pain.

This is insane. Okay, Mom. You said the raven's your totem. That's how you followed me. How you protected me. I guess we share the same power. My most powerful spell is supposed to find you... It's supposed to save you. How is that the thing that activates the heron coin?

She puffed out a sigh and kicked up a spray of sand with her toes. "It can't be like...an evil spell, right? But everyone in that club in Canada was terrified of it. No one wants me to use it. What's going on?"

The sun glinted off the ocean and made her stop abruptly. She turned toward the breaking surf and the salty air. *At least something feels familiar. This smells like home.*

After another deep breath, she exhaled slowly and tried to release all the tension that had coiled inside her since she'd ripped herself out of the Black Heron network. "It shouldn't matter what kind of spell it is. Everyone else is afraid of it. That has to count for something. It means I have a chance at this."

The words on one of her mom's notes ran through her mind. *The only chains that truly bind us in life are the ones we forge ourselves.* It was a weird warning, especially when she'd opened the wooden box at Melissa Bore's house and read this message right around the time she'd freed Romeo from literal chains. Now, though, it made more sense.

"She gave me that coin for a reason." She nodded at the clear blue sky above the Black Sea. "She knows I can handle it. Romeo knows I can handle it. And I..." She closed her eyes and clenched her fists. "I'll simply forge more chains if I back out now. Do what you've always done, Lily. Practice that spell. Master it. Use it. That coin's only a tool, not a definition of who I am. There's always more than one way to open a lock. The black cloud and my raven might as well be lockpicks, right?" A few spoonbills fluttered and darted into the surf, oblivious to the witch at war with her conscience only a few yards away.

"Don't hold back," the old Romani woman had told her. "You know your greatest power now. Use it when you have to. Use all of it." The Ochiului had known what she could do, even if they didn't know how or what she was.

"I'll discover that part too," she muttered. "Yeah. And right now, I'm wasting time."

Lily turned and headed back along the beach toward

the Winnie. The illusion dome she'd cast around her home on wheels—and Romeo's too now, after everything they'd been through—was very well done. The sand on the beach was too coarse for her to follow her footsteps all the way back, so she clapped as she walked and summoned the pink, filmy spell between her palms. When she drew her hands fully apart, the rest of the spell activated enough with a faint pink flash to show her the vehicle and the dome of her illusion. She snapped her fingers and shut the new spell down before it fully exposed them again to anyone who happened to drive past this stretch of beach on the highway. They were isolated there, yes, but the coastline south of there was studded with resort after Romanian beachfront resort. Someone was bound to notice something if she wasn't careful.

"And I'm not trying to operate like the Black Heron." She stepped inside her illusion dome and the air shimmered around her until the Winnie appeared in full view. "They cast spells and kill magicals for the whole world to see. I'm close, Mom, but I gotta be smart about it." She opened the side door, stepped inside, and found Romeo seated on the small couch behind the driver's seat.

He looked at her from where he leaned over his lap with his forearms resting on his thighs and another mug of coffee nestled between both hands. "I honestly thought you'd need more time than that," he said, his eyes wide with surprise.

She shrugged. "Well, I've always been a quick thinker. You know that." He chuckled. "I guess taking a walk to clear my head isn't any different. And I still have work to do." She strode toward the short hallway and the bedroom at the back of the RV while she shook both her hands out to prepare for it.

"Woah, hold on a minute." He stood but she didn't turn. "What are you gonna do?"

"The Black Heron saw me in the network. It might be only a few hours before they begin to appear all over the beach. I probably have less time than that to find my mom first. I'm going back in."

THREE

"Okay... I need to make sure I have this right." Romeo grimaced at the relic in his hand like it was a scorpion about to strike him. "Three minutes and then I... what? Push you away?"

Lily smirked at him as they sat cross-legged on the bed, facing each other. "Maybe try a gentle nudge first, huh? If that doesn't work, you can throw me across the room."

"You know, as fun as that seems in my head..."

She snorted. "Please don't throw me."

"I only hope this thing doesn't blast me through the wall or anything. We still have a good stash of your mom's gold left, but it would suck to have to use it all on a new fridge or something." He tried to smile, but his nostrils flared so much in distaste at the feel of the heron coin in his hand that his lip merely twitched instead. "It's a bad time for jokes, isn't it?"

"Only if they're bad jokes." Neither one of them laughed. "Yeah, okay, it's a bad time. I set the alarm." She placed her phone beside them on the comforter. "Are you ready?"

"Are you?"

"Well... At least I know what to expect this time."

He nodded. "Then let's do it."

Once she'd tapped the start button on her phone's alarm, she stretched toward the silver coin in Romeo's palm and this time, set her hand on it firmly and decisively. The same sensation seized her—a blinding flash, a pull like someone had vac-sealed her lungs, and complete darkness. Her rigid muscles faded, followed quickly by any sound or sight or the feeling of her own heart pumping in her chest to leave her with the disconcerting but now familiar nothingness.

The red lines appeared much faster than the first time and streaked out from wherever she was at the center to form the complicated grid of thousands of the Black Heron Society's members. *It'll probably become easier and faster each time but I definitely don't plan to use it that much.*

The voices and the faces that appeared from every corner of the darkness almost overwhelmed her but this time, she knew enough of what to expect. She took a deep breath—or at least she thought she did—and tried to ignore all the other society members in the network. They reacted to her in very much the same way and stopped whatever they were doing to look up or turn to sneer at the young witch who'd entered their domain unwelcomed and uninvited.

Where are you, Mom? That was where she had to focus and she deliberately pushed all other faces from her mind and turned her complete attention to the memory of Greta Antony's face as she'd last seen it. The most recent memory came from her vision in the Ochiului crypt—her mom had pushed herself off the floor and turned toward the candle on the table while she somehow watched. Her hair had been matted and stringy and her cheeks gaunt beneath heavy, exhausted eyes.

Apparently, that was all it took. She lurched through The Black Heron's network while the red lines and blue-tinged faces burred past her. *This looks like warp speed—* How could she possibly think about Sci-Fi movies right now? The flashing blue and red morphed into a tunnel ahead of her. It all still moved quickly but slowly enough now for her to see. Trees and mountain ranges flashed past her, all tinged blue, but none showed her either magicals or non-magicals—nothing she recognized. The tunnel images streaked down a long, isolated highway and through multiple towns. If she had been more connected to her body, she might have been sick when the magical corridor dropped out of the sky and onto a wide road. It was now as if she looked at everything through the Winnie's windshield.

The images slowed barely enough for her to glimpse a highway sign for Oitylo before she was whisked farther to a seaside town of squat, boxy buildings cut into the cliff face and the mountains farther inland. At that point, the movement ceased as if the tunnel's controlling force had skipped ahead on a video. Now, she saw a room made entirely of stone—no windows and, from her viewpoint, no doors. It was eerily like the room in which she'd seen her mom a few days before when the Romani eye made of blue fire had given her the vision she'd needed.

Only this time, there were five people in the room instead of only one. Four of them formed a semi-circle around a dark shape on the floor, their backs turned away from Lily. One of them stiffened and tilted his head as if to discern something he sensed.

Mom...

Greta Antony knelt on the dark stone, her shoulders hunched and her wrists heavy at her sides with the chained manacles clamped tightly around them. The woman raised her head and although her eyes were closed, she smiled. "Good."

The man who'd obviously felt Lily's presence in this strange, member-locating network whirled and locked gazes with her. "I see you too," he muttered. "We all see you, Lily. Now, you have nowhere left to hide."

Greta's eyes snapped open although she obviously couldn't see her daughter herself. "Go!"

One of the other society-members who stood over the woman delivered the back of his hand in a vicious slap across her cheek. Greta fell without a sound, and despite how much Lily wanted to hurl the assholes through the stone walls, she'd seen what she'd come to see.

When she thought of the heron coin sandwiched between her and Romeo's palms, she considered yanking her hand away. It happened instantly—the blue-tinged view of her mom's current prison and captors disappeared and was replaced by the sight of his open palm and the flashing silver coin he held.

Her hand jerked away with so much force, she almost toppled off the back of the bed. His free hand darted out to catch her other wrist, and he pulled her slowly toward him with a sigh. "Are you okay?"

She swallowed as he released her and she nodded slowly. "Yeah. I found her."

"You did? Okay. That's good. I guess you don't really need me to pull you out of there, after all, do—"

The alarm on her phone went off. Despite the supposedly calming ringtone, he recoiled from it with a startled shout. The relic leapt from his hand and thumped against her pillow. She jabbed a finger onto the screen to turn the alarm off quickly, and they sat in silence for a few seconds while they tried to bring themselves back under control.

"Not that time, no." Her voice sounded really loud in the silent bedroom although she'd intended to say it quietly. "Who knows? I might need you next time."

Romeo leaned toward her over his crossed legs and widened his eyes. "Next time?"

"Which I really don't think we're gonna need." She shook her head. "I saw more than enough."

"Your mom?"

"Yeah. A town called Oitylo." She snatched her phone and pulled up the Internet app, but all she had was the *No Internet* screen. "What?" A glance at where her service bars should have been showed *NO SERVICE* in all caps.

"Lily?"

With a sigh, she rolled her eyes and settled her gaze on his worried expression. "No service."

"We've been in the same place for two days. Your phone worked yesterday, right?"

She shrugged. "I guess my bank account's running on empty now. Either that or someone else disconnected my phone deliberately. Which feels like a useless thing for anyone to do."

"Yeah, it's not like that would stop you from finding anything out if you can simply use the coin."

"It's definitely inconvenient but not really a problem I need to handle right now, though. Can you..."

"Oh." He straightened and nodded. "Yeah. Give me a sec." He turned to crawl off the bed, paused for another glance at her, then stood and headed toward the front of the Winnie.

Lily rubbed her cheeks and stared at the silver heron coin that now glinted on her pillow. "No more sleeping with that thing out in the open," she muttered.

Romeo stepped back into the bedroom with his head bent over his phone. "You said Oitylo?"

"Yep. I guess my translator spell works in...dark-magic tunnel vision, too."

"Tunnel vision?"

"That's exactly what it looked like." She gestured vaguely. "Where are we headed now?"

"Greece."

"Huh."

He raised his eyebrows and smirked at her. "Yeah, I didn't see that coming, either."

FOUR

"I'm very sure we can make it there in two days." Romeo readjusted his grip on the steering wheel as he turned the Winnie onto E675 to head southwest to Greece.

"That's assuming we aren't stopped along the way." Lily tilted her head and raised her eyebrows at him.

"Right. That's not really an option for us anymore, is it?"

"Romeo, that stopped being an option when we found Rosalía and Filipe on the side of the road."

He smiled at the memory—not of finding two stolen kids huddled in the back of the van but of how smart and strong they both were. And how different. "Stopping to rescue kid witch twins and take them home to a village no one's heard of—wait. Does their village even have a name?"

She grinned and stared out the window. "I don't know. If it does, I never heard it."

"Yeah, that's kinda weird. It was worth it, though. I bet Rosalía would say the same thing."

"About us rescuing her and her brother? Or about being kidnapped?" She shot him a playful frown at how strange it sounded.

"Both, probably."

"Well, I'd do it again, no question. I know you would too."

He cleared his throat. "Absolutely."

"Things are a little different now, though, aren't they?"

"Since Mexico?"

"Yeah." She shrugged and pushed her hair away from her face. "Since getting to Europe, too. For one thing, what we found out in Bucharest was huge."

In response, he raised a hand from the steering wheel and waved it slowly in front of him. "The Black Heron Society seeks magicals of every race and ability to power their 'magic for every evil asshole' spell. Willing and unwilling volunteers accepted."

"Careful." She snorted. "The way those people are headed, it wouldn't surprise me if they actually put out a horrifyingly stupid ad like that. They might as well, with all the spell evidence they've left behind for every non-magical to see."

"That's what the whole Non-Magical Relations thing is for, right?"

Lily shot him an exasperated look. "Not everyone has a Gabriel Mercier to clean up the Black Heron's mess up and wipe dozens of non-magical minds."

"True..." He glanced at her before he focused on the highway again. "But yeah, Lil. Things have changed considerably since we left Charleston."

"You know, it somehow feels like everything's gone full-circle."

"How's that?"

"Well, a witch tried to kill me in a parking garage, for one. I'd bet the rest of our gold coins that the man was part of the Black Heron. Now, we have them all targeting us again. There's no way they saw me in the network and decided not to find me."

"Well, you have me with you now." Romeo looked a little smug. "And we've changed too, haven't we?" He set the back of his open hand on the wide center console between them.

She glanced at his hand, then laced her fingers through his and stared ahead at the highway in front of them. "Yeah. That's one change I'm happy about." *Even the fact that we threw the L-word around a few days ago like we know exactly what we're doing. Maybe we do. It's kinda weird that it doesn't feel weird.*

They drove in silence for a few more minutes before she squeezed his hand. "Hey, I have a question for you."

He chuckled. "Um...you know, that's basically like saying, 'We need to talk,' but asking a question instead."

"Don't worry. I promise you that it's worse for me than it is for you."

"That doesn't really make me feel better, Lil." He laughed. "Whatever it is, you know you can simply ask. I'll always tell you the truth."

"Yeah, I know that." *And that's kinda what I'm afraid of.* She took a deep breath. "I know that heron coin freaks you out. And I know you didn't like sitting there with me when I used it again, even though you didn't say anything."

"Uh-huh..."

"I activated it with that black-cloud spell and my own shadow-bird. The raven that's supposed to be my totem too, or spirit animal, or whatever—"

"Lily, if you're worried about that freaking me out too, I'm gonna shut that down right now." He squeezed her hand in return and nodded. "I know who you are. If your totem spell activated the coin, it's because that raven of yours is as powerful as you are. It doesn't make you one of them."

Lily swallowed and stared at his profile. "It's really creepy that you can read my mind like that."

"Good. And since I can read your mind"—he grinned at her before he shrugged and turned back to the road —"I'll go ahead and say that you're definitely not another lunatic who thinks kidnapping people and sucking the magic out of them is a good way to get what you want."

Despite the fact that the Black Heron literally did exactly that—and no doubt targeted her and Romeo now as well—she laughed. "I do still get what I want, though."

He threw his head back and laughed with her. "Yeah, you do. And it's even better when what you want and what's right are the same thing." One more time, he flashed her that grin. "I'm not worried about you and that coin, Lil. I'm with you all the way. Even when we now have a magical Black Heron GPS tracker riding with us in the adventuremobile. Hey, where did you put that thing, anyway?"

"The coin?"

"Yeah."

She pressed her lips together and tried to hide her smile. "I don't think I'm gonna tell you because I have a feeling you don't really wanna know."

"You make a valid point." He snorted. "As long as it's not where we eat or sleep or...well, anything else, I'm happy."

"Anything else, huh?"

Romeo turned to meet her gaze and wiggled his eyebrows. "We do all kinds of things besides eat and sleep, don't we?"

"Life would be boring otherwise." She rolled her eyes and uttered a chuckle.

"Naw. It's never boring with you, Lil."

And it's about to get far less boring. She gazed out the window at the flat, brown land spread around them and the low mountain ranges to the north. *I only hope we don't get held up for too long. Hang in there, Mom.*

FIVE

They crossed the Romanian border only a few hours after leaving the beach on the Black Sea. Now, driving through Bulgaria felt almost as mundane as driving through the northern deserts of Mexico. A flat, dry, brown vista stretched all around them and they passed only a few small towns on the way.

After five hours straight through, they stopped for a late lunch in the town of Nova Zagora. Romeo had worked his own form of magic with the map on his phone and his eerily quick way of finding whatever they needed faster than Lily expected. With the Winnie parked conspicuously on San Stefano, they gathered their things, stepped outside, and locked it behind them.

"Is it weird that a place I've never heard of in Bulgaria seems nicer than Bucharest?" He stared at the two- and three-story buildings lining the narrow street.

"How much did you really know about Bucharest?"

"Not much." He shrugged. "Things simply look a little...better off here."

"Maybe you chose a better neighborhood." She stepped onto the sidewalk in front of the Coop Mercuiry 12 restaurant he'd chosen and waved him forward with her. "Darius' apartment wasn't exactly in the best area."

"Yeah. Or it might have something to do with the fact that all the buildings are pink."

"Well...I'd call it more of a salmon color."

He finally looked away from the buildings, met her gaze, and narrowed his eyes. "Please tell me you're not one of those people who freak out about calling a color by the wrong name."

She laughed. "I knew that would get your attention. Come on. I'm really hungry, and I also wanna get back on the road as soon as possible after this."

With a smirk, he stepped up beside her on the sidewalk and took her hand. "We could have simply stopped at one of the rare and infrequent gas stations."

"I'm not sure how I feel about gas-station food in a country I know absolutely nothing about. Other than the fact that it's between Romania and Greece and that's why we're here."

He opened the door for her and followed her inside the restaurant. "It can't be that bad."

"You know, for a guy who gets all bent out of shape when there's no meat in a meal, you're shockingly undiscerning about gas-station food." They stopped in front of the small counter a few steps inside the door to wait for someone to greet them.

Romeo draped his arm around her shoulder. "I can't help it. A werewolf needs meat, babe."

She rolled her eyes and fought back a smile. "And you can't help being okay with whatever weird packaged food we'd pick up in a gas station in the middle of nowhere either, huh?"

"That doesn't have anything to do with being a werewolf, though."

"No." Lily wrapped her arm around his waist and gave him a little squeeze. "That's simply 'cause you're a guy. Babe."

He laughed and hugged her closer. "Okay. I'm whatever you want me to be, Lil."

"Good answer." She looked around the small dining room in the café and frowned. Two tables had customers, but she didn't see anyone who looked like they worked there. "Maybe we missed something about how Bulgarian restaurants work. Do you think there's something we—"

"Hi. Hello. Hi..." A young woman who couldn't have been older than eighteen hurried toward them, her eyes wide and her ponytail of thin auburn hair a little loose. "I'm so sorry I made you wait. You two made a good choice to come in after the rush. Please, sit anywhere you like, and I'll be right with you."

"Great. Thanks." Lily grinned at the girl before their hostess-server hurried off again to the kitchen. "Where do you wanna sit?"

Romeo nodded at a two-person table on their left beside one of the tall, narrow windows. "I like windows."

"Windows are good."

They seated themselves and waited at the empty table for the girl to find them again. He inclined his head toward the kitchen. "She's a witch."

She glanced around the restaurant but none of the three other patrons in the bright, white-washed café paid any attention to anyone else. "I know you can smell magic on people," she said in almost a whisper, "but why do you look so surprised about it?"

"I look surprised?"

She chuckled. "A little, yeah. It's not like we haven't run into other magicals all over the world, at this point. Or at least three different continents."

He studied the door to the kitchen with an odd expression, then shook his head. "No, I'm not surprised to find a witch waiting tables in Bulgaria. I only... Well, I can't really decide if I smelled her stressing over more customers or..." He frowned.

"Or what?"

His green gaze flicked up to meet hers. "Fear." She gaped. "It's still hard to tell the difference sometimes. I've had the wolfsbane for a couple of months, right? But I have twenty-two years before that of not being able to smell anything but magic and...well, you know—acting weird about it."

She leaned toward him and smirked. "Yeah, my sense of smell gets messed up too when I have allergies."

"Ha, ha. You're so funny." He rubbed the back of his neck and straightened in the chair to look out the window. "Hey, the patio out back looks nice."

"There's a patio?" Lily stretched over the table and

craned her neck to look at what was essentially behind her. "Huh. I wonder why no one's eating outside right now. It doesn't look like there's a whole lotta shade." She looked at him and shrugged.

"Or maybe it's because she doesn't want this guy to bother anyone." He nodded toward the window again.

When she turned a second time, she saw both their flustered server and a new customer in the middle of a clearly stressful conversation. The woman spread her arms and gestured furiously toward the restaurant. She seemed way too distracted to notice two of her customers ogling the scene from inside. The man who caused her so much distress—dressed in khaki shorts and a white polo shirt—folded his arms in a way that suggested both arrogance and impatience. Whatever he said to her, it made their server shake her head like her life depended on it before she gave the man a dismissive wave and turned toward the restaurant. "That doesn't look like a customer," Lily muttered.

The man's hand lashed out and caught the young woman's wrist hard enough that they could hear her shout of pain and surprise, although it was muted through the glass. "No, he sure doesn't." Romeo flattened both his palms on the table in readiness. When the stranger jerked the server toward him again and ignored her furious and terrified struggle, the werewolf stood abruptly. His chair screeched across the café floor, and Lily bounded from her chair.

"Yeah, this looks like Paris all over again." Her foot bumped the table as they all but ran to the back door that opened onto the restaurant patio. The other patrons gawped at them in surprise, but she didn't care. *What are the chances that this guy's another member of the Black Heron?* She burst through the back door with Romeo at her heels. *Crap. A hundred percent.*

The aggressor stared at the woman in his grasp with a feral grin. Where his hand clenched around her wrist, a red, shimmering glow like hot air over burning coals rose from her flesh. She shouted again in pain and tried to pull away, but his other hand grasped the back of her head and forced her to look at him.

"I've given you more than enough chances, Mihaela," he stated coldly and pulled her closer and closer with another burst of energy every time she fought him. "This is your last chance to accept what I'm offering you—"

"And this is your last chance to take your hands off her." By the time the man's gaze flicked across the patio and he noticed the witch and the werewolf who stood a few yards away, Lily had already summoned a roiling ball of flame in her hand. He sneered at her but still didn't release his captive from his grasp. She tilted her head in warning and tossed the fireball once before she let it flare in her palm again. "I bet you mine hurts more."

"You have no idea what you stepped into," the man retorted. He paused, glanced from Lily to Romeo and back again, and his eyes widened. "Oh, I know who you are. You're the little witch who stumbled into a great big spiderweb, huh?" He chuckled. "Everyone's coming for you, little witch. You know that, right?"

"Well, I'll deal with them too when that happens. Let her go."

"No. Mihaela and I have a few more things to discuss, don't we?" He jerked on the server's hand again and she cried out in pain and attempted to pry his fingers from her wrist.

Romeo growled, stepped forward, and his eyes flashed silver like they always did before a shift, which usually served as enough of a warning. "You're fairly stupid, aren't you?"

"Not as stupid as a werewolf who dares to fight any of us with the kind of magic we have in our possession." The man sneered and narrowed his eyes at them. "You wouldn't be able to handle yourself."

"Try me."

During their little standoff, the server had recovered her wits enough to release a shimmering streak of yellow light from her palm. It struck her captor squarely on the underside of his chin, and he roared in pain and surprise and lost his hold on her. Everything else happened at the same time.

The frightened witch darted to the door to the restaurant. Lily unleashed her ball of fire and it rocketed toward the man's chest. He ducked and spun away to run but Romeo growled again and loped in pursuit with the speed only a werewolf could reach, even without transforming. He tackled his quarry and pinned him on the white flagstone of the patio, a knee in his chest and one hand clamped around the society member's throat. Lily summoned her physical compulsion spell with a tight fist and restrained the man's hands after she'd stretched his arms out as far as they would go without dislocating a few joints.

He jerked his head up and hissed in Romeo's face. The werewolf snapped at him and put enough pressure on the man's throat to make him choke. She hurried toward them.

Romeo had better keep it together. The last thing we need is a front-page headline—American Werewolf in Bulgaria.

When she reached them, she brushed her fingers quickly across his hunched back to remind him of where they were, who she was, and who he was. His muscles twitched under her touch but it worked enough that he eased his hold on the man's throat a little.

She stood over the member of the Black Heron Society —the first one they'd seen up close and personal since knowing who the group was and what they wanted. The prisoner wheezed a laugh. "It's useless," he said derisively. "There are too many of us to hunt, witch. And we'll constantly appear when you least expect it."

Lily studied his face and confirmed that she hadn't seen him before, either in their travels or in her brief moments within the society's magical network. She squatted and leaned over him as close as she dared. "I wasn't hunting you at all. You merely happened to inter-rupt our lunch. But I guess I could thank you for it 'cause we're gonna have a little talk now." She glanced at Romeo, who still breathed heavily and bared his teeth at the man pinned beneath him, despite the fact that he remained in human form. *That sounded like I actually plan to torture this guy. If he believes it, I guess that's all that matters.*

"You can talk all you want." The man tried to laugh,

but Romeo's hand pressed so forcefully against his throat that it came out as a gurgling croak. "I won't."

"Why is the Black Heron after me?" She opened her hand again, and the man's eyes glistened green with the reflection of the crackling electric sparks she summoned. He studied her attack spell for a moment but merely shot her a cold grin. "At first you wanted me dead. A witch tried to kill me in Charleston. But you admitted that the others are coming for me. Why?"

"We're almost there, you know. And you're gonna help us."

She scowled at him. "What's that supposed to mean?"

"Poor little witch." The man gurgled another laugh. "You're clueless and all alone without your mommy, aren't ya?"

Now they're bringing my mom up too? She worked hard to not let her surprise show. "I know far more than you think." She brought the crackling green sparks closer to his face. His eyes widened only a little, which made her focus a little more closely. Thin, green-black lines snaked up his skin from beneath the collar of his shirt. "What?" She stood and stepped back to take in the whole picture. The man's fists were clenched where her spell kept them pinned away from him, and a dark energy pulsed within those fists. Green and purple and black light alternated in quick succession, and the green-black streaks like poisoned veins had already covered both his arms. "What are you doing?"

Their prisoner wheezed another laugh as Romeo noticed the transformation too. The werewolf loosened his hold and his hand jerked back in reflex when he saw the serpentine tracks that oozed over the man's flesh.

"Hey, stop it!" Lily twisted her other wrist and used the compulsion spell to open his hands. The pulsing, sickly lights faded, but the man simply continued to laugh. *It's too late to stop whatever spell he cast.* "Romeo..." She took another step back and gestured for him to join her, although he couldn't see her as his gaze was fixed on the eerie spectacle. Thankfully, common sense clicked in and he stood of his own accord and backed away from the cackling witch, mesmerized by the tendrils of blackened veins that covered his visible flesh.

The Black Heron witch drew a rattling breath and grinned and his eyes rolled wildly in his head. "It looks like you're out of options again." His head rocked from side to side on the white flagstone of the patio, and his gurgling chuckle was abruptly cut short. A thick black column of energy with purple sparks blazed from his mouth directly into the sky.

It was over in two seconds. All that remained of the unknown spell was a puff of purple smoke, so dark it was almost black, that escaped from the man's gaping mouth and took the last of his breath with it.

"Did he..." The werewolf dragged in a deep breath and squinted at the body.

She swallowed. "Yep. Wanna bet that's the Black Heron's version of a cyanide capsule?"

He turned to look at her with wide eyes, the silver of an impending shift now gone and replaced by his natural green flecked with gold. "I definitely didn't expect that."

"Yeah, these people apparently think their secrets are important. I assume he thought I'd be able to pull the information out of him eventually."

"Could you?" Romeo shrugged and cast another glance at the corpse, every inch of the man's flesh still covered in those black, slinking lines like veins. They weren't likely to disappear, either. "If it came to that, I mean. Do you think you could've made him talk?"

When he looked at her again, Lily didn't think she could answer that question right away. All she could do was shrug and they didn't have to say anything to know they shared the same guess. With whatever power her black-cloud spell carried—and whatever fueled her own raven totem exactly like her mom's—there was probably a good chance that she could have used it for a successful interrogation. *And that's exactly the kinda thing I'm trying to avoid.* She fought a shudder.

"I can't believe this." They both turned to see their server standing outside the door into the restaurant, her arms clasped tightly around herself as if in a hug. Her eyes were wide, and her gaze remained fixed on the dead witch's body. "What happened?" She looked at them with terror and grief and a plea for these two strangers to answer all her questions.

The couple exchanged another glance, and he nodded with a tiny shrug. She turned toward the young witch who hadn't even had the chance to take their order and offered her a small, cautious smile. "I think we can spare a little time to talk you through it. You might wanna go check on your other customers first, though."

The woman stared at her, glanced quickly at Romeo, and turned to enter the restaurant door. She paused to look at them again over her shoulder before she hurried inside to do as suggested.

He rubbed the back of his neck and stepped toward Lily, trying not to glance at the dead society member's body every few seconds. "Do you think she'll stick around to hear what we have to say?"

"She will if she wants answers. I know I would." She sighed. *I still do.*

SIX

"This is so much than I thought it would be." Romeo nodded at the round *banitsa* pastry in his hand, speaking around a mouthful, and Lily shook her head.

"I'm glad you're enjoying your lunch."

"Huh?" He wiped his mouth with the back of a hand and looked at her from the passenger seat of the Winnie. "Sorry, I... You said you weren't hungry. Do you want some of mine?"

She shook her head and readjusted her hold on the steering wheel. "No, thanks. I'm still not hungry." Glancing quickly at him, she couldn't help another smile as he leaned over the to-go box in his lap and tried to keep all the yogurt and eggs that dripped out of his pastry in one place. "It's kind of amazing that you are, actually."

"Well—" He stopped to give himself time to chew and nodded exaggeratedly as if that would make him chew and swallow faster. "Think about it. We managed to save the first magical who was about to either be kidnapped or killed by the Black Heron, so that's a win."

"Kind of a win." She shrugged. "I really would have liked to make him talk."

"I know, Lil. But it's better that Mihaela's alive so she can talk. All things considered, I'd say that worked out fairly well."

She inclined her head slightly to concede the point and scanned the highway ahead of them on their way across Bulgaria. "Yeah, we were lucky, I think. What are the chances that the first witch we save from those creeps has one of Bulgaria's top magical chancellors for a dad?"

"I didn't even know there were magical chancellors." He took another huge bite.

"Honestly, neither did I." She couldn't help it and glanced at him again only long enough to see another lump of food drop from his mouth into the to-go box. "I thought I knew enough about the Council before all this. But at least the man had enough contacts to help clean up the guy's body without making too much more trouble. Hopefully."

"Do you think being a chancellor's like being with the Non-Magical Relations Department?" He sniffed and wiped his mouth again. "And yeah, before you say anything, maybe I have fixated on what Gabriel Mercier does for a living." She chuckled at that, and he looked a little sheepish as he studied what remained of his food. "It simply feels like... I dunno. Even with the Council and all these countries we've been through, they feel really disconnected, you know? Like no one really knows what's happening."

Lily nodded and thumped her hand a few times on the steering wheel. "They should."

"That's what I'm saying. What if there was a way to connect everyone again? Or maybe for the first time. Who knows? It might make dealing with the Black Heron a little easier."

"You know..." She hunched forward and frowned out the windshield as she put all the pieces together in her head and realized that he'd raised a very valid point. "I can't believe I didn't think of that before."

"Well, you kinda did. You mentioned trying to put Gabriel and Darius in contact at some point, right?"

"And I seriously considered doing that but only after we find my mom."

"Maybe it's worth more to do it now." Romeo crumpled the wrapper of his Bulgarian pastry and tossed it into the to-go box before he closed it. "You never know. It might help us. Kinda like a giant, international version of Ichacál."

She grinned at him. "I honestly would never have compared the two like that. But you're right. None of us would have fought together if we weren't all down there trying to escape from the Wisemen."

"Exactly." He belched, looked surprised, and pounded his chest. "Sorry." She merely rolled her eyes playfully and focused on the road. "But that's what I was thinking, anyway. The only thing—at this point, anyway—that connects all these countries we've been through—Mexico, France, Germany, Bulgaria, and everything between—is the fact that the Black Heron doesn't care who they snatch as long as they get to steal someone else's magic." He frowned. "Well, I guess the Council connects everyone too, in a way. They're worldwide, right?"

"Yeah." Lily shrugged. "At least, they're supposed to be. But it's not like they're doing anything about the Black Heron or this monster spell they're trying to power."

"Do you think the Council even knows?"

"At this point, I really hope not. They'd have so much to answer for if they knew what was going on and never raised a finger to help any of the kidnapped magicals or even try to eliminate the Black Heron. And if they really don't know, I have a feeling they will soon enough."

"Probably, yeah." He stretched his arms above his head, tapped his fingers on the roof above him, and released a huge yawn.

"Are you tired now too?"

"It's probably only a food coma." He patted his stomach and crossed one foot over the other beneath the dashboard.

"You and food." She shook her head again and fought another laugh. "Literally no matter where we are or what we saw—"

"It's not all the time, Lil. Yeah, I like to eat." He smirked. "But for the most part, we settled everything fairly well in Nova Zagora. Mihaela didn't become another magical in the Black Heron's living reliquary. Her dad sent guys to clean the place up after the witch made a mess of... well, himself. And we were able to explain to a few more people with some kind of influence what's really happening. Whether or not they believe us and wanna do anything about it is up to them, right? But it feels like we played our part. After the last couple of weeks, it feels kinda nice to know we did something to help someone again, you know?"

"Yeah, I get that. I do." Lily sighed. "The last time we were really able to help someone... Well, like I said, things were different. Now I know where my mom is. Getting her out of there feels like the only part I should play."

Her words pulled him completely out of the sluggishness that had descended after he'd finished his entire meal in under ten minutes. He straightened in the passenger seat and rubbed her shoulder to encourage her. "And that's exactly what we're gonna do, Lil. We both know that."

"Yeah. We will." She held her hand out and he laced his fingers through hers. With a quick glance at their hands resting on the wide center console between them, she took a deep breath and nodded at the highway and their straight route—for now—across Bulgaria toward Greece. "What I'm stuck on is what we don't know. Like when the next society member's gonna take a stab at...whatever it is they want from me."

"Careful what you wish for, right?"

She knew he had only attempted to lighten the mood a little. Through everything they'd experienced—all the weird magical crimes and terrified people and inexplicable fights they'd gotten themselves out of—he had been good at that. So far, it still worked. She let herself smile and squeezed his hand.

THEY STOPPED in Zlatograd that night, which was big enough for them to buy a decent grocery list of things one always wanted on hand in an RV—most of it being toilet paper, toothpaste, bottled water, a few packaged snacks so they didn't have to stop as much, and a couple of frozen things they could cook on the way. One of these—an oddly labeled package that really didn't make sense with Lily's DIY translator spell but had a picture of pasta and chicken on the front, she hoped—currently warmed on the stove while she and Romeo settled in for the night.

"So it's been, what? Almost twelve hours since you used the coin?" He crossed his legs in the spinning armchair behind the passenger seat.

She stirred the pasta one more time, let it sit for a few more minutes, and leaned against the kitchen counter. "Something like that." She smirked at him. "I don't think it's really possible to time attacks by the Black Heron."

He glanced at her from his phone and smirked. "Okay, now I think I've heard everything."

"Oh, yeah?" She chuckled.

"I thought I heard Lily Antony tell me something's not possible. That can't be right, can it?"

With a smirk, she pushed herself off the counter and walked toward him. "I didn't say it was impossible. But it's not a very practical use of your time to try to predict what these people will do, or when, or how. This isn't like mapping another road trip."

His expression suggested that he was genuinely startled by the realization that he couldn't approach these two things in remotely the same way. "There's gotta be some kinda trick to it, though."

"A trick?"

"Okay, not the best word choice." He held her gaze as she stepped between his legs and moved his hands to hold her hips. "But you said using that coin is like a network, right? Some kind of tracking system where you could see every member and where they were and what they were doing."

"Not every member."

"Right, but still. It's like a system. And as much as I hate to bring her up at all, that old woman with the Romani witches said that once you used the coin, you'd be like a beacon to the Black Heron."

"She said something more like a bonfire in the night."

"Even better." He squeezed her thighs as if for emphasis and she pursed her lips and waited for him to continue. "A bonfire doesn't instantly appear out of thin air. It takes a little time to build first and eventually, it burns out."

"That depends on what kinda bonfire we're talking about. If it's a normal one, yes. You're completely right. But seeing as this whole thing is about magicals and taking their magic to fuel a ridiculously dangerous and definitely illegal super-spell... I'm gonna call this one a magical bonfire."

He stared at her for a moment before he pulled her down into his lap with a playful growl. "You're completely missing the point."

A small laugh escaped her as she straddled him in the

armchair and slipped her arms around his neck. "No, I'm not. I'm only trying to be realistic."

"So am I, Lil." He held her waist and kissed her softly. "So bear with me, okay? Magic has its limits too."

"I can't argue with that one."

"Good. I'm merely trying to see what the limit is on the heron coin. And the only way I can think to do that is... well, yeah. Make a timeline."

Lily hugged him closer and kissed him far more deeply this time. Her fingers slid up to play with the dark curls at the back of his neck, and before she could let herself drift away in the feeling of being with him, she smelled smoke. "Do you—" She jerked away from him and caught sight of the pan on the stove and the thin trail of smoke rising from their almost-ruined frozen dinner. "Crap!" She bounded off his lap and ran the few steps across the Winnie to slide the pan aside, turn the burner off, and stir what she could in the pan so it didn't all end up as one crispy, neglected lump of carbon.

He burst out laughing.

"You know, I'd think you'd be a little more concerned about what happens to this...uh, whatever it is." She stirred quickly and poked the charred pieces stuck to the bottom of the pan before she retrieved two plates from the cabinet. "Seeing as this is dinner for both of us."

"I wondered how long it'd take you to work that one out."

With the plates served, she set the pan in the sink and turned toward him with wide eyes. "You knew it was burning?" He merely raised an eyebrow. "Of course you did. Why didn't you say anything?"

"Come on, Lil." Romeo spread his arms in the chair and flashed her a brilliant grin. "A beautiful witch on my lap kissing me like that? It's probably the only thing I'm not gonna turn down to get in a good meal."

She tried to look stern, placed a hand on her hip, and brandished the serving spoon as she squinted at him. *Literally nothing looks better than that smile.* That was all it took to break her down, and she finally laughed at him and shook her head. "Well, I can't promise this is gonna be a good meal. But if you don't mind a little blackened...man, I really hope that's chicken."

"It's weird that it doesn't say on the package, right?"

Lily pulled two forks from the drawer, set them on the plates, and took those to the two-person kitchen table. "My translator spell's not the best with every language, apparently." She slipped into the booth and didn't try very hard to hide her smirk as Romeo joined her. "Seriously, though, I smell smoke, and my brain instantly goes to—" She couldn't finish. *So now I have problems talking about Mom and her shadow-bird, huh?*

He nodded and set both forearms on the table before he leaned toward her. "I know. You haven't seen your mom's shadow-bird since the Ochiului. I wouldn't read too much into it, Lil. You did see her in the network. That's all we need to know right now."

"Yeah. You're right." *I only hope that the next time I have to use the heron coin, if there is a next time, I can still see her*. She smiled at him and dug into the steaming plate of chicken and pasta in front of her.

Romeo chewed thoughtfully for a few seconds, then pointed at his plate with his fork. "You know, this really isn't that bad. It has a nice, crispy flavor."

She pursed her lips and flicked her finger ever so gently at him as he lifted another forkful. The mouthful he'd planned to take leapt from his utensil and plopped onto the plate again with a wet smack.

He looked at her with wide eyes. "Okay, remember what happened the last time you did that? You started a one-way food fight."

"I'm more focused now." She grinned.

"Yeah, yeah." With a nod at her plate, he scooped up another forkful. "Focus on your own food."

SEVEN

They were up early the next morning and only had to drive about an hour and a half before they crossed the border from Bulgaria into Greece. "You said two days, right?" Lily leaned forward in the passenger seat to look out Romeo's window and that side of the windshield. The mountain range surrounded them on every side and the trees and the greenery looked calm and bright in the morning sunlight.

"Yep." He nodded. "Two days as long as we don't get held up too much. We almost reached the halfway point last night and have another..." His gaze flickered down to his phone in the cupholder. "Eleven hours."

"That's totally doable."

"For sure." When he glanced at her again, he flashed her a reassuring smile.

She leaned back in her seat. "I realized I have way more of a problem with waiting for someone to attack us than actually being attacked. We can handle that, no problem. Expecting it to happen is merely exhausting."

He snorted. "You only now realized that?"

"Yeah." She cast him a sideways glance. "It's not like I've spent any length of time waiting for some seriously dark magicals to spring out of the woodwork in a foreign country before they blast spells at me." His quiet laughter was still contagious. "Why is that so funny?"

"It's definitely tense. I get that. But it's funny that you're surprised by not liking the waiting part."

"Again, Romeo. Why?" She couldn't wipe the smile off her face, despite the fact that she felt like she'd missed the punchline.

"You don't like waiting for anything, Lil—not magic and not the next clue when we were still looking for those instead of your mom. Patience isn't one of your strong suits at all and never has been."

"Why do I feel like we've had this conversation before?" She squinted at him.

"Because we have."

"Okay, that simply means I need a distraction."

"Well, I'm a little busy driving right now." He smirked.

"Oh, cut it out." Lily eyed his phone in the cupholder and decided now was as good a time as any to make the call. "Can I use your phone?"

"Uh...sure."

"I'm gonna call Gabriel and let him know what's going on." She grabbed his phone and typed in the passcode— five-four-five-nine. Something about those numbers tickled a memory in the back of her mind—one she couldn't quite grasp but that felt like a puzzle piece on the verge of falling into place.

"Are you okay?"

When she realized she was frowning at his phone, she shook her head and nodded. "Yeah. I was...remembering the guy's card is..." She stretched forward to retrieve her purse from the center console between the cupholders. "In here somewhere." She rummaged around between all the odd, random things she'd shoved into it at one point or another. *It's hard to believe I actually kept Mom's first clues in here. And hard to believe how little I actually use a purse anymore.* Gabriel Mercier's business card played hard to get, and with a sigh, she snapped her fingers and waited for the yellow flash of her location spell to do the work for her. The small piece of cardstock flipped from its hiding place and whisked itself into her open hand. "Got it."

"See what I mean?" Romeo tipped his head toward her and kept his eyes on the road. "You are not very patient."

"It's not being patient if I literally can't—never mind." She ignored his laughter, fought her own smile, and dialed the number for the French witch with the Department of Non-Magical Relations.

"Mercier."

"Hi, Gabriel?"

"That's right."

Lily glanced at her companion and quickly set the device on speaker. "This is Lily..." She realized she hadn't given the man her last name—neither of them had—and right now, that might have been safer for all of them. "We met in Paris a few weeks ago after a certain...uh, incident outside the creperie."

"Yes, I remember." The man cleared his throat. "I honestly didn't expect to hear from you. But I'm glad you called."

"That's good to hear."

"What can I do for you, Lily?"

"Actually, this might be more about what we can do for each other. I'm not sure how much you'd be able to help us now, seeing as we're...relatively outside of France."

The magical detective grunted over the phone, which sounded remarkably like he tried not to laugh. "So you're still lying low, huh?"

"Mostly, yeah."

"And still not ready to tell me what you're really up to?"

"Actually, that's why I called." Romeo gave her a reassuring nod when she glanced at him, and she lowered her hand with the phone onto the center console to make it feel less like a one-sided conversation somehow. "Like I said, I'm not sure how much you can help us right now, but I hope you'll be able to help many other people. That part's important."

"I can't promise you anything, Lily. Other than that, I'll do what I can with whatever information comes my way."

"Well, I guess that's enough." Gabriel Mercier's muffled chuckle rose quite clearly over the line, and she felt a little better about having this conversation now that the ice was broken. "I should probably warn you that this is... Well, things might become a little more dangerous for you once you know what we do. So if that changes your mind at all—"

"Every single day of my career has been a little more dangerous than the last, Lily. I'm actually really intrigued by your call. So please, say what you called to say."

"Right." *It sounds like I'm stalling, doesn't it? But at least this way, there's a chance to keep a few more magicals from getting hurt.* "Romeo and I have learned what that symbol of the bird in the circle means. The heron."

"Go on."

"Have you heard anything about the Black Heron Society?"

"Unfortunately, no."

"Okay. So we have to start at square one." She rubbed her temples and cleared her throat. "It's a society of magicals unsanctioned by the Council, first of all. They're behind most if not all of the magical kidnappings and murders you've dealt with over the last few months. And it's not only happening France."

"Do you have any proof of this?"

She shrugged, then remembered he couldn't see her. "Most of that is with us right now. And we're...on the move. But I know someone who can fill in more details for you than I can. With proof."

"A name would definitely be appreciated."

"The man's name is Darius. I...didn't get his last name, actually. But I have an address."

"I'm ready when you are."

"Good." She smirked at the image in her mind of Gabriel Mercier trying to sift through the connections when he heard what she said next. "How quickly can you get to Budapest?"

"He took that fairly well," Romeo said.

"Well, at least he was gracious enough to make it sound like he took me seriously."

"Come on, Lil. You heard the man. At this point, he's willing to follow virtually any lead he can get."

She stared at the black screen of his phone in her hand and nodded. "We sound like we've lost our minds."

"I don't think so. Hey, if there's anyone who can convince people of something they don't wanna hear, it's you."

Lily glanced at the ceiling and let herself chuckle a little, simply because it was easier. "I guess this is good practice for when we get my mom home and start resolving all the damage from whoever faked her will. That's a plus."

"Definitely."

"And we can start getting to work on the whole 'equality for werewolves' thing." She nudged his arm with the back of her hand.

"All right. Easy, counselor."

"Hey, I think I'd make a fairly decent lawyer. If I wanted to go through that much school."

He nodded and shifted in his seat. "I don't think anyone can argue with you there, Lil. Case in point, right?"

"Hey, that reminds me..." She rifled through her purse again and located her own cell phone—which, at this point, she was sure had been disconnected because she hadn't paid her bill. "One more call. Do you mind?"

"Nope. Who's next?"

"Bentley. I'm hoping I can get my phone turned on again. And I haven't talked to him much since we left Charleston and feel kinda bad for not checking in. I should probably have done that when you called your dad before we got on that freighter."

"I'm surprised Dad hasn't called me more, honestly."

Lily found Bentley McClure's number in her phone and dialed it on Romeo's, hoping her mom's long-time friend and personal accountant picked up a call from an unknown number. *I'm reasonably sure my overdue phone bill is only an excuse.* The line rang once. *He deserves to know I'm okay after everything he did to help me. I probably won't tell him what we've done to the Winnie until after—*

"Bentley McClure."

"Hi, Bentley."

There was a long pause before her family friend uttered a high-pitched laugh of surprise. "Lily?"

"Yeah. How are you?"

"How am I? Wow. Lily, how are you? It's been months."

"I know. I'm sorry, we—"

"No, no. Please don't apologize. I'm so happy to hear from you. Are you all right?"

"Yeah. We're good but...still working on finding her."

Bentley cleared his throat. "Sure. Listen, I know you probably can't talk about much of it over the phone, but... were you right, at least?"

"I was." She nodded, her certainty made even stronger when she remembered how unsure everyone else around her had been when she'd first started this whole search. "I was definitely right. And we're really close."

The man's shout was so loud through the phone, she had to pull it away from her ear to keep from going deaf. *I have never heard him make that sound.* She couldn't help but laugh as she listened to what had to be Bentley McClure, CPA, stamping around his office and pumping his fist in the air as he hissed, "Yes,'" over and over again. She could clearly picture it.

"That's incredible, Lily. I'm simply... I knew you were on to something. You had to be after you called me about"—his voice lowered to a whisper—"four-fifty-two. But even that helped you, right?"

"Definitely. We couldn't have gotten this far without you."

"Oh, that's not true at all. But I am more than happy to have pointed you in the right direction, one way or the other."

"Well, as far as I know, we're still heading in the right direction. So that's something. Bentley, I really want to tell you everything, but that probably has to wait until we come home. All three of us."

"Of course, of course. I understand."

"I only wanted to make sure you were okay and let you know that we're—"

The rippling crack of a lightning strike blasted through the Winnie like a huge, thick sheet of metal. It was indeed a particularly violent surge of lightning, only it hadn't come from the sky at all. The first of the Black Heron members had finally caught up with them.

EIGHT

"Shit!" Romeo braked wildly and the vehicle fishtailed across the fortunately empty highway. His phone careened from Lily's hand and up against the windshield as everything else around them was hurled in the same direction. Her purse scattered its contents all over the dash, dishes crashed together in the cabinets, and she distinctly heard the zipped duffel bag full of her mom's spellbooks slide out from under the bed at the back and thump against the bedroom wall.

The RV slid to a halt on the highway with tires squealing, and for a fraction of a second, everything was still. She whipped her head toward him. "Are you okay?"

"Yeah. You?"

"There's nothing like a seatbelt. Why did you stop?"

"It was mostly a knee-jerk reaction. But I also didn't wanna try to outrun anyone in this thing, especially when we can simply..." He jerked his thumb behind him with a quick tilt of his head.

"Yeah, good point." They unbuckled their seatbelts and stood quickly from their seats, which weren't damaged but would definitely require cleanup. That would come later.

She summoned her favorite attack spell of blisteringly hot, bright red sparks and let the first round of it build larger than normal in her palm. As she approached the side door, she glanced at him. He had already stripped his shirt off and his fingers yanked the belt from around his waist quickly.

It's probably a good idea if I—"

"Yeah, please do." She nodded curtly and turned toward the door again. *I can't remember actually seeing him shift from beginning to end...stop. There are more important things right now, Lily. Like who the hell tried to rip the Winnie apart.* She moved down the two steps toward the entrance as his growl switched midway from rather human-sounding to entirely wolf. It seemed like a good idea to wait a little longer in case the Black Heron members had something else up their sleeves. *Which they most likely do.*

Romeo lowered his head behind her and bared his teeth, his shaggy black fur only adding to his massive size as a wolf.

"Here we go." She pushed the door open slowly and nothing happened. Cautiously, she shoved it a little wider, stuck her head, and out and saw nothing. "Okay, this is really starting to annoy—"

The crashing rumble came from the back of the Winnie, and this time, the dark witches' spell—there were most likely more than one, if she judged correctly from the impact—shoved the RV along the cracked asphalt of the highway. Despite being in park, it skidded forward several feet, and she leapt out to avoid being thrown around inside her own home.

The soles of her flats skidded on the road shoulder. Before she could actually fall, the hand she hadn't filled with flaring red sparks hastily cast a single pulse of heavy force. It helped her regain her feet, and that was all the time she had to consider what to do next before Romeo bolted past her. His massive paws scrabbled across the asphalt as he snapped and snarled at their attackers.

Yep. Definitely more than one.

There were three, actually, and they all looked ready for a fight.

The witch who'd sent her own massive spell of electric energy lowered her hands from where she'd aimed them at the Winnie as the werewolf reached them. The other two magicals who'd joined the hunt for their prize fanned out. The woman lowered a hand toward his shaggy black form, and Lily delivered the first burst of her attack spell.

The aggressor, of course, had to choose between defending against the incoming wolf or deflecting a magical assault. With a wave of her hand, she diverted the red spell toward the other side of the highway and sneered at the young witch. "There's no point in fighting this." She raised both hands as if to scoop something up from the ground, then flicked her hands in Lily's direction with a massive shove. The asphalt ripped and crumbled and huge chunks erupted into the sky as the rest surged in an undulating wave toward her target.

The young witch darted aside with time to spare before the wave of highway reached her and she frowned at the woman responsible. "That's a little excessive, don't you think?" Both her hands erupted with red sparks again, and she strode toward the trio in the middle of the highway. *It looks like the Black Heron definitely has teleporting under their belts. They didn't drive here in a car.*

Romeo snarled and leapt at the bald man whose skin had an eerily gray tinge to it—almost purple. The witch—if he could even be called a witch with skin like that—roared almost as fiercely as if he'd shifted himself. His eyes flashed a blazing, electric purple, and an electric jolt in the same shade flared from his fingertips with his next spell—and from his eyes. The werewolf was fast enough to twist out of the way and avoid most of it, but a puff of smoke rose from one of his hind legs when a streak of purple energy singed his hair. He spun and darted across the highway again, moving in a blur almost impossible to follow.

Lily paused at the sight of the man's magic bursting quite literally from his eyes. "That's new."

"We've...experimented." The woman's blonde hair was pulled so tightly into a neat bun at the back of her head that Lily was sure that was the reason for the other witch's incredibly wide eyes. "Would you like to try for yourself?"

"Are you crazy?" She ducked when a massive spear of ice hurtled toward her and Romeo's dark form bounded behind her. They were both too fast for the spell, but where the ice-spear landed, the shattered parts spread into a frozen pool on the asphalt. She glanced at it once to make sure it wouldn't spread any farther toward her while she circled with the other witch focused on her.

Romeo's snarl cut the moment of silence and one of the men attacking them uttered a muffled scream. *Yeah, he's got this.*

"You know, for the kind of entrance you made coming up on us like that, it seems very much like you're stalling."

The woman's grin was predatory and oddly plastic-looking—again, probably due to the tightness of her bun. "You're worth far more to us alive and fully...intact."

"What's that supposed to mean?" She raised her hands again and let the crackling red sparks flare to life in warning. "I'd like an actual answer this time."

"You'll help us complete the circle." The woman stepped slowly toward her.

"Yeah, I've already heard that one before. It doesn't mean anything." One of the other Black Heron members' spells went wildly off course across the highway and yellow flames dripped like thick sludge from the torpedo-like missile that streaked over the asphalt. Either Romeo had clamped his jaws around the guy's arm, or the excited witch thought flaming sludge would be fast enough to use on a werewolf. *There's something seriously wrong with these people.*

"It's really very simple." The woman licked the edge of her front teeth and flicked her fingers toward her. A coil of squirming black rope-like snakes and grasping hands combined spewed toward the young witch.

Lily simply obliterated them with one of her attack

spells while the other flared in her hand, and the danger was apparently over. *It's like she's only learning how a witch-fight works.* She stared at her adversary but didn't let her guard down yet. *Or like she's wasted. Maybe I can use that.* "Okay, let's pretend for the fun of it that I'm fairly simple too. And I need a clear explanation of what the hell you're talking about. Why are you after me?"

"To complete the circle—"

"I know that part," she shouted. *What's wrong with her?* "What I want to know is why me? What's the circle for? The Black Heron's snatched magicals for months now—"

"Years." The witch snarled and swiped a hand through the air. That time, at least, she had a fairly decent command of her magic. The invisible force she'd summoned thudded against Lily's shoulder and hip from the side and caught her completely off guard.

She stumbled sideways and barely managed to stay on her feet. "So what's happening now? You people already have my mom. Why were you sent after me?"

The woman stopped, straightened, and barked a laugh. "No one sent us to do anything, you idiot. If we want to finish what we started, if we want to be whole again after the sacrifices we've made... Well, you're the only one who can do that for us."

Lily shook the hair out of her eyes. "So you only want my help, huh? After all the other magicals you've kidnapped and tortured and murdered, you simply need a little favor to get the whole society back up on its feet?"

"Not exactly." The witch's eyes flicked away toward Romeo behind her.

It was an automatic response on Lily's part. She turned to make sure he was okay and saw him barrel into the man with the grayish skin who somehow cast spells out of his own eyes as well as his hands. As soon as her head was turned to look over her shoulder, a blazing-hot chain wound painfully around her ankles and jerked them together quickly. She went down hard on the asphalt, skinned her hands, and landed painfully on her hip. When she turned to her attacker, the crazed woman held the other end of the chain, which sparked up and down its length with yellow and red wards.

"That was so easy!" The apparent victor shrieked in amusement. Her head raised to utter another wild shriek while both hands clenched around the warded chain. It tightened around her ankles with each second and dug into her captive's skin.

The rest of it happened too fast for Lily to process it. She saw the third society member stalk toward Romeo, who snapped his deadly jaws over the face of the man with the gray skin. The third witch—or whatever he was—chuckled and summoned a shimmering black spear in one hand. More of the dripping flames oozed from the speartip. Her ankles flared with pain and the magic that had always been inside her surged to the fore.

Her hands clapped with brutal force and the sound echoed violently across the highway, even though there was nothing else around them to return it. She jerked her hands apart and no longer fought to contain the power of whatever her black-cloud spell really was. With a thunderous roar, the dark, churning magic built between her hands where it rolled and expanded like a violent storm on fastforward. In only a few seconds, it was large enough to blot out everything around her, and all she saw was the billowed shadow and the silver streaks of energy that coursed through it. The power demanded release and she complied.

"That's in—" The woman's voice rose above the magical storm before the black cloud exploded from Lily's open arms. It careened down the highway and washed over all three of the Black Heron members who'd come to claim their prize and failed. One of the men screamed. The woman shrieked again, no longer in laughter, and a harsh yap of surprise rose over all of it.

It was over as quickly as she'd summoned it. The attack elevated and evaporated to leave three limp bodies on Greece's E90 in its wake.

"Holy crap," Lily muttered. "Did I—"

A sharp, warning bark issued from Romeo's throat as he darted toward her, all black fur and huge paws and glowing silver eyes. He passed her completely and headed directly toward the Winnebago.

"Hey!" She struggled to shove the chain off her ankles. It had already begun to lose its yellow-orange glow. After another push, her feet slipped through the coils and she turned and pushed to her feet. "Romeo, what's going on?"

He shifted from wolf to man in mid-run and skidded to a halt beside the open side door. "Come on, come on!" As he waved her toward him, his gaze darted constantly over her shoulder toward the man with the grayish skin who was, in fact, still lying motionless on the highway.

She looked over her shoulder only once and saw the society member's body—from his huge black boots to the top of his bald head—flare with purple sparks. Understanding her companion's urgency, she sprinted to the RV. He waited for her to dart up the stairs first, leapt in after her, and slammed the door shut behind him.

NINE

"What did you do to him?" Romeo didn't even bother to put his clothes back on. He scrambled over the center console and slid buck-naked into the driver's seat.

"What do you mean, what did I do to him?" Lily stared at him with wide eyes and climbed into the passenger seat. "You're the one who knocked him over."

"Yeah, but he didn't start sparking like that until you did your cloud thing." He strapped himself in, jerked the gearshift into drive, and thrust down on the gas pedal with his bare foot. The Winnie lurched forward down the highway with another squeal of tires and what sounded like a rather resistant groan from the engine. He leaned toward his window to peer into the side mirror, then put both hands on the steering wheel and held them tightly.

She strapped her seatbelt on as quickly as she could and stared at him. "Seriously, Romeo. Why are you so freaked out?"

His gaze strayed constantly to the side mirror. "Is it possible for a magical to...oh, I dunno. Turn into a bomb or something?"

"What?" She startled and frowned.

"Is it?"

"That's, like...the weirdest thing you've ever asked me."

"Yeah." He nodded. "It's even weirder that I'm fairly sure that's what—"

A massive explosion flared behind them. The second one was even louder, and the driver-side mirror reflected the purple glow of the magical detonation on the asphalt. Romeo's profile darkened in the purple glare, and she jumped and twisted automatically to see it for herself before she remembered the Winnie didn't exactly have a back windshield. "Did that guy actually explode?"

He gritted his teeth and squeezed the steering wheel even tighter. "Hold on."

"For what?"

Her question was answered by the giant shockwave that pounded into the back of the vehicle, even after he had already brought them up to almost seventy miles per hour. The RV shuddered, rocked by the double thrust of both explosions and pelted by excess magic and probably extra debris. She turned her head slowly to stare out her window. *Yep. A shitload of debris.* Purple light streaked past them at incredible speeds and carried pieces of uprooted highway, a few scrubby bushes from the shoulder, and what looked like a boot along with it. The Winnie jerked forward a little, but he had managed to bring them to a high enough speed that it wasn't nearly as violent as it could have been.

The eerie glow faded quickly, and she glanced into her own side mirror. Thick columns of smoke rose from the road behind them and she thought she saw a crater in the asphalt, although she couldn't be sure. A few pebbles and blasted remnants of dry plants skittered in their wake, and she turned slowly to her companion. "He did. That guy actually blew up."

Romeo scowled through the windshield for a few seconds before he spared her a quick glance. "Do you wanna hear the weirdest part?"

"An exploding witch who fired purple spells out of his eyes isn't the weirdest part?"

"I smelled it coming."

Lily literally couldn't think of a single thing to say to that.

"Your black cloud knocked him out. I think it caught the others too. That bald guy was definitely unconscious, at least. Then, he started to spark, and I...I totally smelled it. And that is something I never wanna experience again."

"No kidding." She swallowed. "I can only assume it was really awful." He snorted. "And yeah. That definitely counts as the weirdest part."

They were silent for a few minutes, each lost in their own startled thoughts. Finally, he took a deep breath and glanced sideways at her. "Nice job with the black cloud, though."

"Huh?"

"It looked like you really had a handle on it."

Once she got over her surprise at that statement, she grinned. "Well, thanks. I didn't exactly plan it that way. It kinda...happened."

"Well, I think you should let it happen more often."

"Romeo." She spread her arms and wished he didn't have to focus on the road so he could look at her. Then again, she was glad they'd left that part of the highway behind them. "I can't simply let this magic out whenever I want—"

Very slowly, he turned his head to meet her gaze and raised an eyebrow. "I think you just proved otherwise."

"Okay, but it's dangerous. We both know that. Maybe I can use it whenever I want, but it's not a good idea."

"It's the best idea we've had in the last few days, Lil. Who knows how many more of those creeps are gonna target us? Everyone makes it sound like it's about to rain Black Heron members, so I'll stick with my original suggestion that you use that black cloud as much as you have to. It's like a Fatal Blow."

"A what?"

"You never played Mortal Kombat?"

A laugh burst from her mouth before she could even think about stopping it. "No, I never played Mortal Kombat. This is starting to feel too much like a videogame, though, I'll say that much."

Romeo smirked. "I bet you would've leveled up back there."

"Stop it."

"Maybe got some sick new gear."

"Romeo..."

"Or at least leveled one of your abilities or something."

"You're insane." She shook her head and tried to focus on the long road ahead of them.

"Well, I am driving a magically blasted Winnebago Adventurer bare-ass naked, so you might have a point."

That made them both collapse with laughter, and when she watched him in the driver's seat—despite what they'd narrowly escaped and the fact that yes, he was driving naked down a highway in Greece—she felt far better about the whole situation. *That still doesn't change how weird that was.* "Hey, did you notice anything off about those magicals?" she asked when they'd both calmed again.

"Ooh...that's a loaded question."

"No—okay. Forget the purple sparks and the guy shooting spells out of his eyeballs." Romeo grunted in an effort to restrain more laughter. "That woman didn't even really attack me. It was like she kinda played around."

"These people are only trying to catch you, right? To complete the circle or whatever they want you to do. I'm sure some of them might if they had the chance, but I don't think any of them want to kill you."

"Right, I know that. And it makes sense, but the way she threw spells at me... It was like she'd only now learned how to do it on her own. And she wasn't nearly as skilled with her magic as many of the people we've had to deal with."

He frowned. "Yeah... The other guys were actually slow too. I assumed maybe they hadn't gone head-to-head with a werewolf before."

"But the Black Heron brings in every kind of magical, don't they?" She rubbed her forehead and brushed her hair away from her face. "Did you hear her say they'd been experimenting?"

"No. On what?"

"I have no idea. But..." She took a deep breath and let it out slowly through gritted teeth.

"But what, Lil?"

"It sounds ridiculous."

"It can't be any more ridiculous than the last hour."

She sent him a sideways glance and pressed her lips together. "Right again. So bear with me. What if they've experimented on themselves?"

He narrowed his eyes in thought and chewed on the inside of his cheek. "We're talking about a bunch of Frankenstein's magical monsters, here, aren't we?"

"Maybe."

"Okay, I suppose it would explain why a dude with spell-casting eyeballs spontaneously combusted after your dark cloud cleared them out for us."

Lily nodded. "Yep. His skin was weird too. Which might or might not have anything to do with it. I don't know for sure, though. That witch spouted stuff we've already heard like them needing me to complete the circle. That I'm gonna help them. All of it. It sounded like rehearsed lines she simply regurgitated. But she did say they wanted me still intact."

"That's not creepy."

She shook her head and leaned it back against the

headrest. "All of this is creepy. Probably because we're not seeing the whole picture."

"I'm fairly sure the whole picture's gonna be creepy too."

"Well, yeah. That's a fair point." She smirked at him, and he chuckled. "But it makes sense, right? If these people who attacked us today were the Black Heron's inside experiments—like the first dose of the massive spell they're trying to cast—it obviously hasn't worked very well. It's as if they're still missing something important."

"Like you?"

"And I will help them with that over my dead body."

"Well, that's not out of the question with these people." Romeo looked at her and caught her warning glance. "Come on. I'm not saying that's actually gonna happen. But I don't think anyone in that weirdo cult is too concerned about your well-being—case in point with the whole spontaneous combustion thing." He jerked his thumb over his shoulder to emphasize the point.

"Except for the fact that she said they wanted me alive and intact. She also said no one sent them. That might simply be the way the network works with the heron coin. Or...I dunno. Maybe those three were only experiments gone wrong and they heard that Lily Antony is the one witch everyone else is trying to snatch for themselves." She straightened her shoulders, leaned forward, and tipped her head back until the tight spot in her spine between her shoulder blades popped. "Man, I landed hard. That might really hurt tomorrow."

"Are you okay?" He frowned at her and gave her a sweeping glance.

"Yeah. I'll be fine. The crazy witch lady lassoed me or something."

"Seriously?"

"With a chain."

He chuckled. "Okay, that's one I haven't heard before."

"Laugh it up. She sure did." Lily couldn't help snorting a laugh at her own rather dry joke. Romeo merely shook his head and leaned back into the driver's seat so he could straighten his arms. "Please tell me there was something weird about that other guy."

"Not Sparky, right? The other guy?"

"This conversation is ridiculous."

"Well, it fits." He nodded and tried not to think about the fact that he was starting to get a little chilly now that they were out of danger and he wasn't so hopped-up on adrenaline and the rush of shifting. "But the other guy? Uh... Okay, his spells were more like weapons than magic. I think all of them were...drippy."

"You know, oddly enough, I know exactly what you're talking about." She rubbed her shoulder where the witch's summoned force had shoved her over like a playground bully. "That was weird. And if we're right—if this is three for three with the magicals who might have experimented on themselves— Well, I guess I don't know what. This keeps getting weirder."

"And, of course, we keep going down the rabbit hole, don't we?"

She bit her lip, placed her hand on the center console,

and wiggled her fingers. He slapped his hand playfully down on hers and laced their fingers together. "We do. I don't think I'd want anyone else to fall all the way to the bottom with me."

"Nah." He offered a little shrug that almost looked embarrassed but kept his one hand firmly on the steering wheel and his gaze focused on the road. "We always land on our feet."

TEN

They stopped three hours later at a tiny gas station only long enough for Romeo to put his clothes on. Laughing, Lily cast the purple light of her illusion spell around the Winnie's windows for his benefit but she didn't bother to look away when he stood from the driver's seat and went to collect his clothes strewn all over the floor.

When they were back on the road, they had a little over four hours left in what they both hoped was the final leg of their trip.

"So we're gonna find her in Otiylo," Romeo said and nodded slowly.

"Yep."

"Did you see that town? As in clearly?"

She looked at him and chugged the last of the bottled water she'd opened earlier. "Are you getting nervous?"

"No. Definitely not." He chuckled. "I merely wanna make sure that we're heading in the right direction, you know? 'Cause at this point, it feels—"

"It feels like we're almost at the end of this whole thing, huh?" She raised her eyebrows at him and tried to hold back the wild grin that threatened to break through. *Don't get your hopes up too much, Lily. Four hours is still more than enough time for things to go wrong.*

"Yeah. That's exactly what it feels like." He cleared his throat. "But if you say Greta Antony's in Otiylo, Greece, that's exactly where we'll go. And we're gonna kick some Black Heron ass when we get there."

She honestly couldn't help herself. "Not if they all blow themselves up first."

They both laughed, and he shook his head. "It'd be nice if the heron coin showed you the future, huh?"

"I don't know." She shrugged. "If I saw exploding society members in the network, would we really wanna keep going this way?"

"Is that a serious question?"

"Not really." She smirked. "Yeah, we'd keep going anyway. I did see the future—when I touched that blue eye made of fire."

"Yeah, that was you using your black-cloud spell, wasn't it?"

After a short pause, she looked at him and studied his profile. *He really doesn't forget much of anything, does he?* "Yeah. That. But honestly, I have no idea if what I achieved back there with those Frankenstein witches was the same kinda power I saw in my vision. Maybe I'm getting close. But I'm not sure I want to see much more of the future than that, you know? Aren't there stories out there about how seeing the future only makes it harder?

That we'd want to change it? Or that we'd end up turning it all into a self-fulfilling prophecy?"

"The storyteller Amal saw the future. For both of us."

Lily tilted her head and looked out at the flat ground sprawled all around them with the mountains to the north and the Aegean Sea to the south. "Who knows how much she could actually see? The only thing she did about it was give me a rock."

"She gave me a warning, too. It's still creepy to think about, right? She knew you'd be in that Romani chamber thing underground. And she knew I'd be chained to a tree by betting werewolves."

A soft chuckle escaped her. "Who, apparently, are also part of the Black Heron."

"We sure get wrapped up in a lot of weird stuff, don't we?"

She took a deep breath, leaned against the headrest, and stared at the dashboard. "I used to think that, yeah. But I can't really ignore the fact that now, it simply feels like all this was planned somehow. We know where my mom is and I'm still missing a huge piece of the puzzle."

"Huh." He puffed his cheeks out with another sigh. "Maybe it's your mom."

"She probably would have more answers if I could actually talk to her for longer than a minute or two. But we wouldn't be driving across Greece right now either if we weren't trying to get her out."

"Self-fulfilling prophecy." He gave her a reassuring nod and looked surprisingly confident about the whole thing. "I'm starting to think we can handle anything."

"Well, we're not done yet."

THEY REACHED the outskirts of Otiylo a little after 7:00 p.m. as the sun dipped below the closest hills ahead of them. "It must be nice to get to see the sun rise and set over the ocean every day." Lily stared out the windshield as the sky exploded with pinks and oranges and purples and spilled the same colors across the Mediterranean Sea.

"It's like that back home in Charleston." Romeo pushed the visor back into place.

"Not like this, though. Well, maybe only for the people who live on Folly Beach. They don't have anything else in front of them but ocean, either." It wasn't the first time she'd thought of home since they'd left or even since they'd ferried the Winnie all the way over to Europe. But it was the first time she thought she missed it. "I might be getting a little homesick, honestly."

His eyes were wide when he glanced at her, and he broke into a grin. "Really? You? The witch who's always been too big for wherever she is?"

"Okay, now you're taking it overboard. There is such a thing as too much flattery, you know."

"I'm not trying to flatter you." He ran a hand through his dark curls and nodded at the highway sign into Otiylo to indicate that they should take the next exit. "There it is."

A wave of déjà vu made her skin tingle. *Part of déjà vu is not knowing where you've seen a thing before, right? I know exactly where I've seen this.* "Yeah, this is definitely what the network showed me when I thought about finding my mom."

"Okay, good. We're in the right place, then." His smile faded after a moment. "Do you have any idea if the other society members know where we're headed?"

"I honestly have no clue. Using that coin isn't... I mean, it's not like reading everyone's minds or anything. I saw them and they definitely saw me. But it's more like...a window? Or maybe like FaceTime." They both snickered. "I don't think they know what the network showed me. It's not like I could see what anyone else in there was planning to do."

"Unless someone in there focused on following you exactly like you focused on finding your mom."

With a frown, she turned to stare at him and waited until he noticed.

"Why are you looking at me like that?"

She tried not to laugh, but their circumstances made it a little ridiculous. "You have this weird way of being really optimistic one minute—so sure that we'll find her and get this done and can handle anything—and then you say something like that."

"Uh...like what, Lil?"

"Unless someone in there focused on following you. That's not very optimistic."

He laughed and shook his head. "Maybe, but it's realistic. If the society members know we're here and why we're here, it's not like we can't handle it. I'm not worried about it and I don't want you to worry about it."

"I'm definitely not worried." She folded her arms and

gazed at the small, squat, white-washed buildings of Otiylo that dotted the mountainside in the cliffs above the Mediterranean. "Maybe we simply have different ideas of being realistic versus being defeatist."

Romeo barked out a laugh, and when she didn't join him, he did a double-take. "Wait, but we're still on the same page about your sarcasm, right?"

Despite herself, she grinned. "Yeah. It's a great tool, right?" Romeo's only reply was another laugh. "Okay, we need to keep an eye out. If there are any Black Heron members here, they'd better be the ones holding my mom."

He stretched his fingers on the steering wheel and when he leaned forward, his green eyes reflected the orange light in the sky. "We're coming for you, Greta."

She nodded. "We're almost there."

ELEVEN

"Okay, so in the interest of not actually knowing where she is—"

Lily unbuckled her seatbelt and shook her head. "Nope. I'm not using the coin again. Especially here. That would merely let them all know we have arrived, and our chances of—"

"Lily?"

"Yeah."

Romeo turned the Winnie's engine off and pressed his lips together in an attempt to maintain a serious expression. "Using the coin is basically the last thing I want you to do right now. Or ever, probably."

"Oh."

"I was only gonna say..." He unbuckled his seatbelt and turned toward her. "We should step out, take a look around, try to find your mom, and keep it...low key, right? Sniff around a little."

She hissed a laugh when he winked at her. "You're the one who does all the sniffing. I'll leave that part to you."

"Excellent. Are you ready?"

"Yeah."

He opened the driver-side door and slid out into the cooling seaside air. She glanced around the front living area of the Winnie, which they still hadn't cleaned after their super-odd attack on the highway. *It looks like someone broke in and tried to loot the place. It's a good thing those boards under the kitchen table hold themselves together. We'd probably have issues with bags of gold coins spilling all over the place.*

"Are you coming?" He grinned at her from the parking lot of the very empty-looking hotel where they'd parked and spread his arms.

"Yeah. I only... Yeah." *It feels weird to not need my purse with me anymore. But I guess I don't need anything else when we're this close already. Only Romeo and my magic.* That put the smile on her face again and she climbed over the center console and the driver's seat to slide the long way down out of the vehicle.

After he locked the door and shoved the keys into his pocket, he turned with a sigh and gazed at the rising and falling rows of white clay houses that dotted the hillsides. "Do you have any idea where to look first?"

"I saw the exit to Otiylo. Then, it basically skipped forward to a room underground. And my mom, of course." She shrugged.

"Okay. It's time to sniff out a few seriously messed-up

magicals. Is it weird that I think I'm gonna enjoy it this time?"

"It's not weird to enjoy something you're really good at." Hearing those words from her own mouth made her stop. *I'm starting to sound like him, now. And I have no idea if that statement applies to me using that black-cloud spell.*

Romeo obviously had the same thought as he sent her a furtive sidelong glance. His brows drew together for only a second before he nodded. "That's very true."

"Hey, did you bring any wolfsbane with you?"

He patted his back pocket. "I learned my lesson, Lil."

"And now, it's a steady part of your diet, huh?"

"It might be the only plant I actually enjoy eating."

She rolled her eyes with a chuckle. "I guess we're as prepared as we're gonna be. So, let's go."

They wandered down the street with sufficient daylight still left, despite the fact that they walked in the shadow of the hills in front of them. It was quiet in Otiylo, with only a few older-looking cars that passed them and considerably more people on bicycles. He looked thoughtful but relaxed. "This is one of those places I could see us coming back to. You know, later. For fun."

The idea was pleasant. She looped her arm through his and tried to look casual while every dark shadow and every shape that might have been a flight of stairs leading underground caught her attention. "You really do like to plan ahead, huh?"

"It keeps me going."

It would've been a fairly relaxing, pleasant stroll as the

road rose up the hill in front of them—if they didn't search everywhere for signs of the Black Heron members and also try not to draw any extra attention to themselves. "Do you think there many other magicals here?" He peered down an alley as they entered the first concentrated area of white buildings.

"Do you mean the kind who aren't kidnapping and killing people and trying to steal the magic out of everyone else for themselves?"

He sent her a sarcastic look. "Yes. That kind. The normal kind. The people we could actually be friends with."

Lily bit her lip to keep from laughing and smiled at a woman who leaned out of the second-story window on her right to pin her freshly washed clothes on the line. The woman's smile was brief but not unfriendly—merely distracted. "I don't know. It seems logical that if the Black Heron's been here for a while with my mom, they probably wouldn't want anyone to know where they were or what they were doing. They'd keep it secret, right?"

"Good point."

"Then again, a small place like this on the coast—if there were any 'normal' magicals here—would make a great...well..."

"Hunting ground?"

"If we put it bluntly, then yeah. I guess."

Romeo narrowed his eyes at a wooden door that opened on the side of a building built into the cliffs. An old man with an incredibly wrinkled face leathered by age and years of salt and sunshine stepped out onto the stone steps in front of the door. He looked at them and offered a little wave, which the young witch and her werewolf companion returned. The man simply stood there as they passed and watched either them or the sunset—or had maybe forgotten what he came out there to do in the first place. "So we're not exactly welcomed by a party or anything, but I don't think people would be even this friendly if the Black Heron had made a mess of things. Do you think any of the locals know about your mom?"

"You're simply asking all the questions I'm already thinking," she muttered. Something flapped heavily in the sea breeze, and she looked up toward the roof of a low building wedged into the cliffside.

A young man stood there and shook out a thick rug before he laid it on the roof and set a simple wooden chair on top of it. He nodded at them but he didn't say anything.

"Does it feel weird that no one's talking?" Lily nodded in response but didn't want to stare.

"A little. One of the guys I worked with back home was like...I dunno. An eighth Greek or something, maybe. But he never shut up about how much his giant family talked constantly all the time. It's kind of ironic, actually."

"So you're trying to say that Greek people normally talk more?" She looked at him with a half-smile that warned him not to push that one too far.

"Hey, I'm only saying what he told me. I've never been to Greece before."

"Okay..." Lily turned to glance behind them, searching for anything that looked out of place beyond the fact that this little town on the edge of the Mediterranean was unsettlingly quiet. "Have you picked up any extra magic yet?"

He shook his head slowly. "Nope. I should, though, right? If your mom's here?"

"Yeah, you should." The breeze blowing inland lifted her hair from her shoulders and she wanted to simply stand there, close her eyes, and let the answer come to her. *We don't have time for that.*

They kept moving uphill through the staggered rows of houses and occasionally smiled at the locals who'd stepped or leaned to peer out of their homes to see who walked through their streets. Finally, she caught sight of what looked like a convenience store. She'd been so used to moving from one city and one country to the next with only the next destination and next clue in front of her, that she almost suggested they grab a bite to eat while they were at it. *Don't forget why you're here, Lily.* She pressed her lips together and shook the weirdness of that urge out of her mind.

A little boy peered at her from the alley between the convenience store and the next house built into another hill behind it. He stared at them with wide, dark eyes, and she raised her hand to wave at him.

A shadow passed over the door to the convenience store, flitted through the alley, and drifted across the boy's surprised face. Her grip on Romeo's arm tightened. "Hey —" The shadow was gone before her companion turned his head in that direction, but she didn't need anyone else to confirm what she'd seen. "There." She pointed down the alley.

"What?"

"Something moved down there. I'm sure of it."

The child's eyes widened even further, and when he realized the strangers in his town were most likely pointing at him, he backed slowly into the alley and bolted.

"Yeah, that doesn't look like he knows something," Romeo grumbled.

"Hey, wait!" Lily sprinted across the uneven street toward the alleyway.

"Lily..." With a grunt, he headed after her.

TWELVE

The alleys were incredibly narrow in the town of Otiylo, and while Lily was fit and rarely had trouble slipping through physically tight spaces, she almost thought she'd lose the boy through a few too-narrow strips between buildings. She squeezed herself past a doorway that was once functional but had since been boarded over. Their quarry turned to look over his shoulder, saw her still in pursuit, and uttered a little squeak. She didn't think he could move any faster, but he did.

"Lily, hold on." Romeo barged past the boarded-up door that protruded into the alley and splintered the old, dry wood. Huge chunks of it skittered across the ground. "Maybe we should rethink this."

She skidded to a brief stop at the end of the alley and looked both ways down the next street before she saw the child racing downhill on her right. Picking up the chase again, she prepared herself mentally to use her magic if she had to—even on a kid. They were too close to finding her mom now. She couldn't let herself hesitate if it came to that.

"Lily!" the werewolf called behind her. Once he'd rounded the corner, it took him almost no time to catch up with her. He placed a restraining hand on her arm. "I don't think this kid has what you're looking for."

"You said he knew something." She panted, her gaze focused on the boy's back as he darted behind another building.

"And I don't smell any magic."

That made her hesitate. She turned to look at him, and the clatter of a metal trashcan falling echoed all around them. It rattled for much longer than it should have and she looked up and saw the boy again. He'd climbed a low clay wall along the hillside behind this row of houses. Now on the rooftop in front of him, he wrapped his arms around a thin woman with dark hair in a flowing dress, who held him in a protective embrace and stared silently at the foreigners.

"My guess is he thinks he's in trouble for something else," Romeo muttered and leaned closer to her ear. "But I don't think he has anything to do with your mom."

"Romeo, I saw a shadow—"

"Did any part of it look like a magic shadow, though?" He put a hand on her shoulder and inclined his head to stare at her to try to draw her attention.

She frowned and turned slowly to meet his gaze. "Not...really."

"I didn't catch any extra magic, Lil. It's a little weird

that I don't get anything at all but I'm very sure the kid's a dead end."

With a heavy sigh, she glanced at the boy and his mother, who ran a hand over his dark head of hair. She lifted her hand again. "Sorry."

The woman merely raised her eyebrows, and the child simply stared.

"Am I that scary?" she whispered as she slid her arm through his again and they resumed their walk, now across the other side of town. The center was at the top of one of the small hills above the cliffs, so virtually every direction was up or downhill.

"I wouldn't say scary." He shrugged. "More like intense. I'd probably run too if you'd chased after me like that."

She gave his arm a playful slap, although it felt forced in the tension that somehow seemed to emanate from all around them. "Okay, so I made a bad judgment call. That happens sometimes. But something still feels really off about this place, doesn't it?"

"Definitely." He tipped his head back to look up at the houses set behind the row on their right, most of them cut into the hillside and nestled between tall trees that rustled in the ocean breeze. "Especially when I can't pick up any magic at all."

"So, what's next?"

"Look at you." A man had walked up directly behind them on the street. The couple turned, and she slipped her arm out of his. The stranger spread his arms and grinned. "You have absolutely no idea what you're doing, do you?"

"Excuse me?"

"You're playing with fire, girl—not the smartest choice." His thick mustache fluttered over his upper lip as he spoke. Casually, he summoned a swirling orb of electric-blue light in his palm and regarded her with a sneer. "But that's not exactly the worst thing, is it? I assume intelligence levels aren't that important, in the end. Only the strength of your magic."

She glanced quickly at her companion and muttered, "Did you smell him?"

"Not until he opened his big mouth." The werewolf squinted at the man and clenched his fists. "Now, I'm simply waiting for him to put his money where his mouth is."

A short silence followed this statement and the man tensed. After a moment, he simply glared at Romeo and took a deep breath. "First things first. Where is it?"

As she took a step back in preparation, Lily summoned her red, sparking attack spell and held it out at her side, ready should she need it. "You're gonna have to be a little more specific."

"The coin, girl." With his free hand, the man flicked a round, silver pin on the collar of his khaki jacket. It flashed under the pressure, and she caught the etched image of the heron with its wings stretched in mid-flight. "That's how you got this far, isn't it? Tapping into the source you will never understand."

Fat chance I'm gonna tell him it's locked in the Winnie with our stash of gold coins. That's the only thing I have left to find my mom—as a last resort, obviously.

"Why do you care about the coin if you already have one?"

"Because it doesn't belong you to you." His tone was cutting and derisive. He stepped toward them, and Romeo uttered a low growl. "Down, boy. I have no problem eliminating you first if I have to. We already have more than enough werewolves. Your kind seem to appear everywhere we look. What's another drop in the pot, huh?"

"All right. How bout this?" She fought not to look away in disgust as the man licked his lips and pulled the overhanging mustache into his mouth before it flicked out again. "If you want the coin so badly, I'll give it to you. After you tell me where my mom is."

"Your—" A childlike giggle burst from the man's mouth, and he leaned forward and looked from one to the other and back again. "The little witch girl's lost and wants her mommy. Why the hell would I know where she is?"

"Because you took her." She stepped forward and the red sparks in her palm flared with extra strength. This guy attempted to run her in circles and it seriously pissed her off.

"Well, that's not true."

"I saw it." She sensed Romeo step beside her and even that small action on his part eased her under control once more. Which honestly was a good thing. She couldn't remember the last time she'd been this angry. "I used the coin and I found her. Right here. The Black Heron has her. You know it and now, I know it. And you'll tell me where she is."

"Oh..." The witch smirked and gazed at the slowly

darkening sky. "I see what's going on. You have no idea how any of this works, do you?"

"I know enough."

"No. Otherwise, you'd realize that I don't give a shit where your mom is or who has her or what you've seen. There's a bounty on your head, girl. I'm here to claim it and get the first taste of all that...special magic you have locked up inside you." The nasty-looking mustache twitched and he grinned and traced his tongue over his uneven teeth.

Lily took a deep breath and ignored the disgusting gesture. *He really doesn't know where she is.* "Then tell me who does know where she is."

"No again." The man chuckled. "I'm taking you with me."

"The hell you are." Romeo snarled and his eyes flashed silver.

With a high, humorless chuckle, the witch—who'd come suspiciously alone to capture the young, powerful witch everyone in the Black Heron Society wanted—focused on her for a moment. She returned the stare but without warning, both his gaze and his spellcasting hand jerked toward Romeo. The blue energy streaked toward him as he shifted and leapt forward, pawing at the clothes he hadn't had the time to remove first. She deflected the spell with a warded shield and released her sparking red attack at the witch a second later. He scuttled aside barely in time to avoid most of it, although a few of the magical sparks grazed the shoulder of his khaki jacket.

"You don't want to fight me, girl," he shouted and

glared furiously at her. But, despite his defiance, he didn't retaliate with another attack.

She conjured two more handfuls of spitting red sparks and faced him squarely. "It looks more like you don't want to fight me. I think you're stalling."

The man scoffed, and while he cast the first traces of a smoky purple haze in his hand, he didn't move to finish the spell this time.

Finally free of his tight t-shirt and jeans, the werewolf crouched low on all fours and snarled, and the thick black hackles on his wolf's back raised from the top of his head to his tail. She stood beside him and raised an eyebrow at the hesitant Black Heron hopeful. "The idiots with dysfunctional magic who attacked me earlier today weren't nearly this scared. But you are."

"You're wrong." The witch stepped forward and drew his arm back to fling whatever purple, smoke-like spell he'd summoned. Before he could release it, a shape materialized in thin air beside him. Startled, he froze, and three more figures appeared out of nowhere.

None of them wasted any time on the ineffectual witch who had first confronted the young couple. The closest magical who'd now arrived turned glowing red eyes upon Lily and jerked a hand out. The spell's thin, dangerously sharp barbs hurtled forward and she had barely enough time to duck and raise another warded shield, which sparked and started smoking when the magical barbs struck. The debris it left behind looked frighteningly similar to the shattered window glass of a car on the highway weeks before when a Black Heron member had abducted the driver from the middle of heavy traffic. It had no longer even resembled glass, and the freezing puddles it had left behind were most likely equally as dangerous as the smoking, spitting puddles of black sludge that rippled at her feet.

"No," the first witch screamed. "I was here first, you bloodless savages."

She looked up again as Romeo launched himself at the witch, who screamed under the black wolf's massive paws and released the spell of thickening purple smoke into the sky. The closest newcomer—and all of them had the glowing-red eyes and deathly pale skin of warlocks—raised a hand and fired the same blast of red attack spell that the group of warlocks had used on her in the mountain forests of Chiapas. She summoned another warded shield and deflected it into the closest white-washed clay home. Huge chunks of the wall sprayed everywhere, and she had to turn her spells to launch the debris away from her.

Another warlock used that moment to step up beside the first. Together, they summoned something that felt way too much like icy fingers that clamped around her throat. She choked, her eyes wide as she wracked her brain for a way to defend against magic she couldn't see and that took two warlocks to perform. Both pairs of their blood-red eyes literally flashed with determination.

"You'll come with us before you do anything else," one of them told her in a voice as cold as the magic that threatened to strangle her. They were impossible to tell apart with their high foreheads and uncannily androgynous faces.

Lily gasped for air and clapped her hands. The black cloud built between her palms, crackled with dark energy, and churned the air thunderously in front of her. Romeo's yip of pain was all it took to distract her.

The black cloud fizzled and her stomach sank. *Did I really miss my chance? This can't be happening.* Her vision began to blur and in the moment when she was sure she would pass out, a bright purple bolt struck one of the warlocks in the gut. He—or she—screamed in pain and anger, and the other lost control of the attack spell and howled in utter fury.

Three more purple streaks caught each of the other three warlocks as she fell to her knees with a raw, burning gasp of air. The next thing she knew, the warlocks and the witch—who lay on his side and screamed while he cradled the bloodied shreds of his wolf-bitten forearm—were surrounded by dozens of magicals.

Where did they come from? Lily gasped again, rubbed at her aching throat, and pushed to her feet.

The newcomers all had dark hair and sun-tanned skin. They weren't particularly dressed like any kind of clan or order per se, but she noticed a strip of bright purple cloth tied on each of them in a different way—around arms, sewn to collars, through belt-loops, or used as bandanas around heads. They continued their magical assault on the members of the Black Heron who'd come to claim the young witch and her werewolf friend.

Spells crackled in a searing flurry of red, purple, and blazing white. She summoned her own red attack sparks in one hand and blue flames in the other while she looked for an opening in the magic barrage and the newcomers who had quickly surrounded them. *It doesn't look like these guys came to kidnap me too.*

Romeo darted in and out among them. He tried to reach the warlocks but continually had to dodge spells at the same time.

A woman with a long, loose braid of thick black hair jerked her fist in the air, and a glowing purple weapon materialized in her hand before she pounded it on the cracked street in the north end of Otiylo. "You came here at your own risk," she shouted and her eyes blazed with a purple light for only a second. Her words echoed back at them ten times louder like they were amplified through a sound system, and the warlocks froze. Even the first witch had stopped screaming. The dozens of magicals who had come to the rescue closed around the Black Heron members and stopped as well.

One of the warlocks—now with an open gash across the cheek—glared at the woman with the summoned weapon. Lily took a second look at it too. *Is that a trident?* "You made a pact," he countered.

"Not with you." The woman pointed the tines of the shimmering purple trident at the vanquished magical and scowled. "It's time for you to crawl back into your holes now." The weapon sparked again with a warning fury.

The warlock who'd spoken growled in anger and in the next second, he vanished. The other three glared at the witches surrounding them and followed suit. The only remaining attacker was the witch, who glared at the purple-adorned magical and still cradled his mangled arm.

"More will come for her," he warned and shot a scathing glance at Lily. "If you let me take her now, you'll save yourselves considerable trouble. Your pact won't protect her forever."

His words seemed to have little effect on the group or their apparent leader. "On my land, within my borders, I will do what I must. You're trespassing." She slammed the butt of the trident onto the street again with a loud crack, and more white and purple light flashed from its pronged tips.

The witch snarled, glared at his erstwhile prey again, and brought his good arm up to the silver heron pin on the collar of his khaki jacket. A dark shadow settled over him and in a moment, he was gone.

The street on the side of the hill fell completely silent, and every pair of eyes turned toward Lily. "Thank you." Her voice was scratchy and weak. *That warlock attack did more damage than I thought.* "However you did it, you showed up at the perfect—"

"Stop." The woman with the trident shook her head and glanced at the darkening sky, where the brilliant colors of sunset were all but faded into twilight now. "We won't talk here. But we can take you somewhere safer than this. Will you come with us?"

She hesitated, her natural caution coming to the fore, then glanced around the surrounding circle of other witches who'd come to her rescue. *They wouldn't help us only to hurt us somewhere private. Would they?* Romeo's paws clicked across the street as he trotted to her side, and when she dug her fingers into the thick black fur of his neck, she definitely felt much better about accepting the offer. "Yes."

The woman inclined her head in acknowledgment, and her purple trident flashed another brilliant purple light before the young witch, her werewolf companion, and all their rescuers vanished from the streets of Otiylo.

THIRTEEN

Lily hadn't known what to expect from the trident witch's teleportation spell. Although it was probably more accurate to say she hadn't expected the spell at all. Clearly, though, that was what had happened. One minute, they stood under the fading light in the salt air. In the next, they were inside, surrounded by smooth, cream-colored walls. Her stomach did a little flip.

"Do you feel like you're gonna be sick?" a man asked and stepped toward her with a smirk.

"I..." She swallowed and forced her stomach under control. "I'm fine. Thanks."

"Sure. But say something if that changes, huh?" He shook his head and walked off, but the smug expression remained on his face.

Beside her, Romeo uttered a low whine and hunkered on the cool floor beneath them. "Yeah," she muttered. "That was rough for me too." She glanced up to see where they were but soon realized it would be impossible to determine that on her own simply by looking.

The room was huge but not entirely rectangular because the walls didn't exactly follow a straight line in any direction. They were the same dirty-white as the houses and buildings of Otiylo built into the hillside. The entire room, though, was lit with soft orbs of magical light that hovered less than a foot under the low ceiling. The few dozen witches who'd come to their rescue milled about. Some of them whispered softly while others silently studied her and the black wolf who lay beside her.

The woman with the long black braid lifted her trident and it disappeared in a muted purple flash. She approached the visitors and offered them a tight smile. "I take it that was your first time teleporting."

"Not exactly." She licked her lips and found them drier than she'd expected. "But like that? Yeah. That was a first."

Their hostess nodded and pursed her lips to try to keep her smile under control. Then, she glanced at Romeo. "How's your friend?"

He snorted in response, and she nodded. "He'll be fine."

"Takis!" The woman whistled to catch the attention of someone in the group of witches gathered in the white-walled room and pointed at Romeo. "Grab some clothes."

"Yeah." A young man wearing a newsboy cap with a purple ribbon sewn onto the short bill hurried off to do what he was told.

The dark-haired woman extended a hand toward Lily. "Cosima."

She shook the proffered hand. "Lily. Again, thank you. I...I'm glad you showed up when you did."

"That's why we're here." Cosima's brows drew together. "I'm not sure why you are, though."

"That's kind of a long story."

"Well, as of right now, I think we have more than enough time for long stories." She gestured at the room around them. "I'd go so far as to say this is the safest place in Greece, for now. Few people know about us down here."

"I hope you're right—" The statement died as a thought intruded. "Wait, down here? Are we under-ground?" Cosima nodded, and her heart fluttered in excite-ment. "I'm looking for a woman with blonde hair like me and blue eyes. She's...well, she doesn't look her best right now, I'm fairly sure. She's being held by—"

Takis skidded to a halt beside them with a bundle of clothes in his arms. He didn't seem to notice the huge black wolf on the floor at first, and he took a hasty step back in surprise when he looked down. "Uh...I hope these work." He stooped and dropped the clothes before he turned stiffly and disappeared again before she could thank him.

"Make sure your friend has what he needs." Cosima nodded at Romeo, who'd raised his head only enough to sniff at the new clothes. "Then we'll talk."

Lily stepped toward the woman. "This is important, though. The woman I'm looking for—"

"Can wait a little longer." Cosima settled a gentle hand on Lily's shoulder. "I have a few important things too, and

they're down here with me. I'll find you when I'm done."
With another tight smile, the woman nodded and left the
couple to themselves without a backward glance.

She wanted to go after her but knew that wouldn't help
her chances of getting any answers. Instead, she sighed and
closed her eyes as she fought to stay calm. "Well, more
waiting, I guess."

Romeo groaned beside her on the floor, hunched as a
naked man now instead of a shaggy black wolf. He gathered the clothes in front of him and shook them out. "That
was far worse than all the jumps we did with Aluino's
people in Mexico."

"I thought the same thing." She looked away from him
and out over the underground cavern—obviously a haven
for—Greek witches, which was as much privacy as anyone
could give him right now while he dressed in someone
else's clothes. "Besides that part, are you okay?"

"Yeah." He stepped quickly into the loose gray trousers
and tugged the long-sleeved shirt over his head. "That was
a super-weird fight, though."

"Tell me about it. Do you think the warlocks were part
of the Black Heron?"

"I can't say for sure but they wanted you for a very
specific reason, didn't they? Whatever that was. I wouldn't
be surprised if they were."

Lily nodded. "So now, the Black Heron has a number
of magicals experimenting with dark magic and blowing
themselves up, plus who knows how many others who are
willing to fight each other to get to me." She turned toward
him to gauge his reaction and released a short burst of

laughter. "All you need now is one of those hats that guy Takis was wearing and you're ready to be in a movie from the fifties."

He spread his arms and glanced at his borrowed clothes. "They're not that bad. Well...I suppose not having any shoes doesn't really help, does it?"

She smirked and shook her head. "Shoes are kinda at the bottom of the list after being rescued by a team of... whatever these witches are. It looks like some kind of secret society."

"Or a group of rebels in a tiny town in Greece." He raised his eyebrows. "Was that a trident?"

"Yeah. It's a little weird, but it did whatever it was supposed to do, I guess." She scanned the cavern for Cosima, but the woman had disappeared as easily as she'd teleported dozens of witches and a werewolf underground. "That was the first time we haven't been able to deal with something on our own."

"It's okay, Lil." He stepped toward her and slid a hand over her shoulder and down her arm. "Needing help doesn't mean we failed at anything. I don't think anything else really matters as long as we're both...you know." His sweeping gesture included them both. "Standing. Walking. Breathing."

Her gaze darted toward him again and she searched his with a frown. "I wasn't."

"I know." Now, he caught both her arms and lowered his head toward her. "I'm so sorry, Lily. Trust me, I don't like it any more than you do that I couldn't...get there fast enough."

She exhaled a long sigh. "It's not your fault. I should have been able to disarm them on my own. If the black cloud is supposed to be as powerful as everyone else thinks it is, I should have used it." *And maybe not let myself get distracted by whether or not he's okay.*

"You're still learning to use it. There's no use in beating yourself up about it. Whoever these people are, they showed up at the right moment and no one was hurt."

Lily pressed her lips together and tried not to smile. "Except for that shrieking witch with the mustache."

"Hey, you know what? He's the one who put his arm in my mouth. Even if I felt a little bad about that, it's still not my fault." They stared at each other for a few seconds before they chuckled quietly. Grinning, he took both her hands and gave them a little squeeze. "Really, the only person I care about getting hurt is you, Lil. So, I'm sorry."

"Don't be." She stepped forward, wound her arms around him, and rested her cheek against his chest. "Things are merely very different than I expected now if we need a group of witches we don't know to arrive at the last minute and fight our battles for us."

"Hold on." He pulled her away by the shoulders and lowered his head again to hold her gaze. "No one's doing anything for us, Lil. We've already had many people fighting with us when they can. That's what this is too."

"You sound like the very first message my mom left me." She bit her lip. "'You've never needed anyone to do anything for you. But remember how important it is to find those people who will drop everything to do something with you.'"

Romeo raised an eyebrow. "Do you really think Greta Antony would leave a cryptic message for anyone that wasn't relevant for all eternity?"

She snorted. "True. I simply thought I would have found all the answers by now, you know. That I could handle all this on my own. It's not like she left messages for anyone else."

"You know, as much as I'd love to see you go up against the entire Black Heron Society on your own, Lil, that might not be the best way to go about it. For anyone."

"You don't think I could take 'em?" She smiled but part of her was less sure about the answer than she had been an hour before.

"No, I know you could. The point is that you don't have to."

Her eyes closed and she tipped her head back and sighed again. "I guess you gotta keep telling me that a few more times, huh?"

"Lily, I'll tell you whatever you need to hear for as long as you still need to hear it." He grinned again and shook her playfully by the shoulders. "And then nothing can stop you."

She shrugged teasingly out from under his hands and pressed her palm against his chest. "I do have the best sidekick."

He pursed his lips and shook his head. "After everything we've been through..." She chuckled. "I'm fairly sure I deserve a promotion."

"Oh, yeah? To what? Associate?"

With a tilt of his head, Romeo rolled his eyes like he

hadn't given it much thought at all. That wasn't exactly true. "Partner sounds nice."

Lily opened her mouth to utter a witty retort, but she couldn't find one. "Partner has a few different meanings..."

"Oh, I know." He smirked and wouldn't release her from his green-eyed gaze. "I'm only puttin' it out there."

"I'll think about it." She smiled a little awkwardly.

"Don't take too long—"

"Lily." Cosima nodded at them as she passed between a few of her followers and clapped one man on the shoulder before he went to finish whatever business he'd been sent to attend to. "We have food and a few comfy seats." She smiled and tilted her head wryly. "Or relatively comfy. I think there's a certain conversation we need to have, and I'm curious to find out exactly what it is."

"Me too." Lily nodded. "This is Romeo."

"Cosima." They shook and the woman gestured toward the far end of the massive room. "There's a more private area where we can talk undisturbed. This way."

The couple exchanged a glance before they followed. The long black braid swung from side to side behind the woman's shoulders. *I don't know what I'm gonna do if I don't get some answers about my mom.*

FOURTEEN

The other witches—all of them with stripes of purple fabric pinned to their clothes or tied around arms, legs, and heads—nodded at the couple as they passed through their ranks. No one looked particularly worried or irritated by the newcomers, but only a few of them offered genuine smiles. *That's probably what happens when everyone spends their time teleporting in and out of a bunker. Who knows how long they've been down here?*

In the center of the huge room, they passed a large, wide pool rising from the floor. It was the same dirty off-white as the walls but it had to be something stronger as it was raised on a pedestal like a massive birdbath. Cosima turned, her mouth open to say something else, and she noticed Lily staring at all the intricate figurines carved with great detail into the rim. "That's a scrying pool." She stopped and glanced from one to the other. "It looks like you've never seen one of these before, either."

She glanced at the woman before her gaze settled on

the figures cut into the stone again. "There are a lotta firsts today, honestly. Are those...are those Greek gods?"

Their hostess offered them a half-smile. "At least you know that much. These were here as part of the scrying pool long before my time. But the gods are even older, aren't they?"

"How old is this thing?"

"Old." She shrugged. "If anything else comes up while you're here with us, you might get to see it in action. Right now, it's merely a group of statues around water. Come on." Cosima headed off toward the opposite side of the cavern again, and Lily pulled her gaze away from the scrying pool.

Romeo leaned toward her and bent his head to mutter, "I hope she knows more about the Black Heron than that pool."

She glanced at him and raised her eyebrows. "Yeah, that would be nice, wouldn't it? You'd think a witch who summons a magical trident would have a little more to say." He simply shrugged and they didn't say anything more until they'd joined Cosima against the far wall.

A ring of round, embroidered cushions waited for them, tossed together in comfortable-looking piles. Most of them were purple, but there were a few patterned in gold threads and different shades of off-white. A low table stood in the middle of the cushions, completely empty but clearly there for a reason.

"Have a seat." Their hostess gestured toward the cushions and leaned back to tap a passing witch on the shoulder and mutter something in her ear. The younger woman nodded and hurried away.

The couple sat on one side of the low table, and Cosima lowered herself to the floor on the opposite side. She fluffed a few pillows, stuffed them under her crossed legs, and linked her arms around her knees. "Now. Tell me about this woman."

"She was taken," Lily said and wondered how much of the truth was safe to share. "We're trying to find her. Everything we know led us here."

Cosima tilted her head as if in thought but her expression remained unreadable. "What do you know?"

"That she's in Otiylo, is held underground somewhere, and is in danger. Also, that we're incredibly close to rescuing her from the people who took her."

The woman nodded and ran a hand over her mouth. "And do you know exactly who that is?"

For a minute, she studied the woman while she weighed her options. Romeo took a deep breath beside her but let her make the decision. *There's really no turning back at this point. Everything has to be all out on the table.* "They're called the Black Heron Society."

The other woman startled, then closed her eyes and sighed. "I'm glad I don't have to try to explain those people to you."

"You've heard of them, then?"

"Heard of them?" She uttered a wry chuckle. "We've come face to face with quite a few of them, to be perfectly honest. And we fought a few more of them earlier." She pointed at the ceiling. "Those were merely the outliers.

They're not...incredibly organized. But that doesn't mean they aren't dangerous."

"Yeah, we know." Romeo nodded.

"Then I suggest you call off this two-person search party." Cosima frowned at them. "It's not worth it."

"It's not—" Lily widened her eyes and leaned over the table. "It's the only thing worth anything right now. Do you know what they're planning to do?"

"Yes."

"That they're stealing magic from all the magicals they've kidnapped—which doesn't even include the ones they've already killed—to power the biggest spell I've ever heard of?"

"Because they wish to make each form of magic accessible to everyone. Yes. I know." Cosima leaned forward too now and held Lily's gaze. Her braid fell over her shoulder, and while she tried to keep up appearances, she couldn't hide the edge of fear in her voice. "And I'm telling you, it's too big for you to stop, Lily. For anyone to stop. Your best choice is to forget whoever they took from you and focus on protecting yourself. Because when the Black Heron Society succeeds in what they're doing, there will be even fewer places where honest, well-intentioned magicals will be safe at all."

She inhaled a sharp breath and tried to absorb what she thought she'd heard. "I'm sorry. It sounded like you actually told us to give up and go wait for the end of magic as we know it."

"More or less." Cosima glanced at Romeo next, who merely stared at her with wide eyes.

Protests surged but she straightened on the cushions and tried incredibly hard not to yell. "I thought you said you could help us."

"You assumed I could help you. I told you I would take you somewhere safe so we could talk. Right now, that's the most I can offer beyond the advice I already gave you."

"That's the worst advice anyone's given us," the werewolf interjected, his voice low and gravelly.

The witch's gaze flicked from one to the other again. "You won't get much better from anyone else. Everything's changing now."

"Yeah, clearly. Everyone's losing their minds." She pushed herself up from the cushions. "I will not give up. Not now." She wanted to storm off, but the cushions made it way too difficult when the toes of her shoes constantly wedged beneath them.

Cosima watched her struggle with an impassive expression. "Many of us have lost loved ones to this madness. I understand how hard it is to accept that this woman can't be helped now—"

"She's not merely some woman," she shouted and stumbled a little over the next cushion when it wobbled beneath her foot. "She's my mom."

The woman took a deep breath. "I'm sorry, Lily. Really, I am. If they've had her for any length of time, though, I'm even sorrier to say that I don't think she can be saved."

"You obviously don't know my mom." She stopped and stared at the woman. "Or me, for that matter."

"They've had her for a long time," Romeo said and

glared at the woman who'd helped them only to turn them down now. "Whatever the Black Heron's doing to all the magicals they've taken, it's not working with Lily's mom."

"What?" Cosima looked up at her with wide eyes. "Is that true?"

"It obviously won't make a difference to you, will it?" Lily looked at him and nodded toward the other side of the cavern. "Let's go."

"Lily, if that's true, it's new information. That changes things." She reached toward the young witch with an outstretched hand. "I want to hear about it. Please."

She glanced at Romeo again, who shrugged. "Maybe they can help," he said. "Maybe not. It might help them, Lil."

"We don't have time for this." She closed her eyes and took a deep breath. "She's supposed to be here."

"If she's here, we can find her." Cosima nodded and gestured toward the cushions again. "But not without knowing all the facts."

I'm not giving up, Mom. I promise. She stared at the woman for a long moment, then lowered herself slowly onto the cushions and forced both her thoughts and emotions into some measure of control.

"Thank you." The woman pressed her hands together. "Start at the beginning, if you would."

Lily stared at the empty tabletop between them. "The Black Heron Society has had my mom for at least six months but she knew they were coming for her. She spent years trying to discover what they were planning and how to stop them before they kidnapped her. The rest of the world—even other magicals—all think she's dead. She's not."

"How do you know?"

"Visions. Dreams. She sent a…her totem to watch out for me. More than once."

"Her totem." The woman frowned in curiosity.

"A raven. I'm fairly sure it's mine too."

"The wise messenger," Cosima muttered. "That's a powerful totem to have."

"Yeah, and it's followed us across two different continents and more countries than I can remember right now." She shrugged. "She left me clues for how to find her in all kinds of different places. And I know she's still alive because I've seen her."

The older witch leaned back on the cushions and shook her head. "It's hard for me to believe that those people would let you go after a talk with your mom." She glanced at Romeo, who grimaced and shook his head.

Lily offered a thin smile. "There's more than one way to talk to someone other than sitting face to face. Shouldn't you already know that with a scrying pool in the middle of your hideout?"

Cosima glanced at the raised pool of white stone, then nodded. "You're right. Is that how you spoke to her?"

"No. I had a vision in a Romani crypt." She tried not to smirk. *Yeah, it sounds pretty cool out of context.*

"Romani?"

"Gypsies," Romeo added.

Her chuckle held a trace of bitterness. "I can tell that you don't believe anything I'm saying. But I swear, that's exactly what happened. My mom even gave me something in that vision. And I don't mean I saw her giving me something and interpreted it. She literally gave me a coin. It's..." *Still in the Winnie. I probably shouldn't say that out loud.* "Well, I had it with me before you guys arrived."

Cosima glanced at the guests in her safe house bunker and a smile flickered at the corners of her mouth. "A coin."

"Yeah."

"And that's how you know she's still alive?"

"Really?" She smoothed the hair away from her forehead. "I don't know why any of this is hard to believe. You summoned a purple trident out of nowhere and fought off a team of warlocks. We're witches. Nothing I've said is impossible."

"No, not at all." Cosima nodded and studied the table between them now too. "Merely highly unlikely. Where did you say you're from?"

"I didn't."

"The US," Romeo said.

The woman's eyes widened. "Are either of you Greek?"

They looked at each other and said, "No," at the same time.

"Well, your Greek is very good."

"That's magic too." Lily looked at the woman. "I promise I'm not trying to start any trouble by making this up. I need you to believe me. I saw my mom held here, in Otiylo, somewhere underground, and we're so close to finding her. Do you know of anywhere in this town where the Black Heron might be keeping her? An abandoned basement, maybe? Or an old jail or something—"

"You saw Otiylo in the vision the gypsies gave you?" Another flicker of fear passed across Cosima's eyes, and it only made her frown.

"Romani. And no. It wasn't that vision."

"Lily." Romeo leaned toward her and raised his eyebrows. His nod was barely visible, but she saw the urgency behind his eyes. "I think we're gonna have to tell her everything. Even about the coin."

"She told us to give up, Romeo. I don't think it matters."

"Whatever it takes, right?"

This is definitely the weirdest position we've been in so far. I thought I was done trying to convince people of the truth. "Okay." She looked at Cosima again and spread her arms. "The coin my mom gave me in that first vision is part of the Black Heron's...network, I guess you could call it. They all have something like it, I think. It might be how they communicate with others all over the world. But I discovered how to activate it and I used it to look for her because I know they have her. That's how I know she's here. I saw her."

The woman's suntanned face drained of color. "And they saw you, didn't they?"

"Well, yeah." She glanced at her companion and shrugged. "That part's kind of inevitable."

"I don't want anything to do with that coin." Cosima's lips pressed together into a tight, thin line. "I really hope you can tell me truthfully that you didn't bring it with you."

"Are you kidding? That's not the kinda thing I feel like carrying around in my pocket."

"Good." The woman nodded but her eyes narrowed. "So now you're going to tell me how you activated the damn thing."

"That's kind of a long story too—"

"Then make it short. The way I see it, you have two answers. The first is to tell me exactly how a regular young witch like you just so happened to activate one of their relics. The second—which is equally as farfetched but who knows, these days—is to tell me that you're actually one of them and you've now managed to scheme your way down here right before all these good magicals lose their lives because I decided to help a few strangers. Which is it?"

"I don't have the coin," she repeated. "You can search me if you have to. And I'd like to think I'd do an awful job of pretending to be part of the Black Heron Society. You're exceptionally good at insulting your guests, you know."

"If that's how I keep my people safe, sure. I'm very good at that too."

With wide eyes, Lily glanced at Romeo. He simply stared, unblinking, at the woman who was apparently incapable of making her mind up about the two young strangers in her hideout. "It's the truth."

"We'll see. First, I want to hear it from you. And then we'll find a way to sort it all out for ourselves."

"Okay, I'm done." She rose again from the cushions and this time, managed to get out of them without stumbling. "I really would like to help you with what I know about my mom. But you're now accusing me of being a spy for the people who literally don't even care that non-magicals watch them kidnap and murder all over the country. They wouldn't have spies, Cosima. They don't need them. And I really don't need to waste any more time giving you answers you've already decided not to believe."

With a low growl, Romeo rose from the cushions too and shot the woman an irritated glance. "All you had to do was listen," he said roughly and followed Lily away from the rear of the hideout.

Cosima stared after them for a few seconds until her shout rose behind the retreating newcomers. "It's won't be nearly as easy to get out of here as it was to get in. Takis! Sandros! We're gonna need the Verity Gage and—"

The scrying pool at the center of the large room erupted with a massive flash of purple light. The water rippled, then bubbled, and a second later, the whole pool leapt up from where it rested in the giant birdbath. The young couple stopped in front of the angry-looking face that now stared at them—the perfectly visible, three-dimensional face made of water that hovered over the marble pool. "Cosima!" The man's watery beard jumped as he shouted and sent a tiny spray of water over the side of the basin and onto the floor at Lily's feet.

"Ozias." At the far end of the room, Cosima stood from the cushions. Every other witch in the underground room paused what they were doing to watch the face and their apparent leader communicate.

"Whatever you plan to do with our guests, call it off."

The face shimmered a little, and beady, watery eyes surveyed the women standing at attention before their gaze settled on Lily and Romeo. "I'll be there soon."

The woman inclined her head in a stiff bow and the magic holding the bearded man's face above the pool released. The water splashed into the basin on the pedestal, and the scrying pool's surface was as still as glass once more.

Lily took another step back until her fingers brushed against Romeo. He glared at the two witches who'd waited for the rest of Cosima's orders and the corner of his mouth twitched in a suspicious scowl. "You'd better forget the Verity Gage, guys." When they backed away, he glanced at Lily and muttered, "Whatever that is."

FIFTEEN

They only waited for about two minutes before a man with a long beard—easily recognizable as the one who'd shouted at them from the scrying pool—appeared. He didn't, however, teleport into Cosima's bunker like the others had. Lily hadn't had time to study the huge room the way she would have liked. Otherwise, she would have definitely noticed that in addition to having no windows and no electricity, the place also had no doors.

She would have also been proven wrong when the large slab of the same thick, white-washed stone receded into the wall itself and slid aside to reveal a hidden passage. The rumbling of it was so loud, it drowned out all the other small conversations held among the witches who had gathered and darted furtive glances toward Cosima. The couple turned as the black passage opened in the wall and Lily bit her lip. "You know, some parts of this are beginning to feel a little like Ichacál."

Romeo stared intently at the open passage. The thick

section of wall slid all the way to the side with a resonating boom. "I'm trying to stay positive about this, Lil. That maybe the similarities stop with secret doors opening into walls."

"Okay. I'll cross my fingers."

The man everyone was waiting for emerged from the darkness of the passage. The minute he stepped into the huge room, he nodded at no one in particular, and all the other gathered witches seemed to take it as an order to return to their own business. His gaze fell on the visitors, and he headed toward them. "I know you've already been here a while," he said and extended his hand toward the young witch. "But I'd like to welcome you all the same."

"Um...thanks." Despite how frustrated she'd been with Cosima, she shook the man's hand anyway. *Maybe this guy will believe us.*

"My name is Ozias." He placed a hand over his heart and nodded his head in what appeared to be a formal greeting.

"I'm Lily."

"Romeo."

Ozias nodded and offered a thin smile. "It's nice to meet you both. I assume you've met my daughter." His quick glance at Cosima, who now walked quite quickly toward them, was all they needed to know.

"We have." She didn't bother to turn and acknowledge the woman. "She and a few of the others here helped us... well, up there." She pointed at the ceiling, not really knowing how far underground they were or what exactly was directly above them. "And we appreciate that part. But

I don't think there's anything you can do to help us much more than that."

He glanced at his daughter again, who stopped a few feet on the other side of Romeo. "Why's that?"

"I'm merely being thorough," Cosima replied, although the question wasn't necessarily directed at her. "The Black Heron has her mother, and Lily says the woman's still alive. She made it sound like she's untouched, too, and said she saw her mom by using one of their—"

"The coin, yes. Thank you. I've already been told everything you know, Cosima. And quite a few things you don't know. You can go."

The woman opened her mouth, paused, and glared at her father. "I'd like to—"

"Not now." His voice cracked through the bunker again and startled everyone into momentary silence. He returned her glare until she sighed in reluctance, eyed the couple with suspicion one more time, and headed away toward the two witches she'd issued orders to before her father used the scrying pool.

Why do I have a feeling she was ready to torture us? Lily watched the woman go and turned to Ozias. "At this point, I think the only thing that could help us is if you knew where the Black Heron was keeping my mother. It's a room underground in Otiylo. That's all I know and the only thing I have to go on."

He stroked his beard once and pursed his lips. "Would you believe me if I told you I've seen your mother with my own eyes?"

She swallowed. "I'd seriously want to believe you, yeah."

"Have you actually seen her?" Romeo asked.

The man merely inclined his head one more time.

"Please." She stepped toward him and forced herself to breathe evenly. "Tell me where she is. You don't have to help me get her out, but I really don't have any more time to waste."

"You have far more time than you think." His brows creased together and he gestured toward the other side of the room at the ring of piled cushions and the low table. "And after what I've heard about you two, I'd say you don't want to go there any time soon. Another few days, at least."

"A few days?" She shook her head fervently. "I don't think you heard me. We don't—"

"You do have the time. Especially if you want to head off after your mother again."

"What do you mean 'head off' after her? She's here."

"She was." Ozias looked at his slightly unwilling guests and pressed his lips together in an expression that might have been regretful. "They left with her this morning."

AT FIRST, when the food had been offered at the small table where they'd reluctantly resumed their seats on the cushions, Lily had refused. Instead, she'd wrapped both hands around the clay cup in front of her, which Ozias had filled with a sweet, floral-smelling tea. "I'd offer you something a little stronger, Lily, and I will. But not before we get a few things out of the way first, all right?"

The tea warmed her belly, which had gone completely cold when she heard her mom wasn't there but had been until less than twelve hours earlier. *Why does this keep happening? What am I* missing?

None of them said a word after that until she was ready to speak. Romeo picked at the plate of moussaka and dolmades a few times, but for the most part, he took her lead and sipped on the tea. He studied her uneasily every few seconds and hoped she could pull herself into determined-Lily mode on her own. She was grateful for the fact that he didn't push her.

"Okay." She lowered the cup of tea into her lap and nodded at the bearded man. "Let's talk, then."

"Good." Ozias reached for a wrapped piece of dolma and stuck the whole thing in his mouth. "This is what I know, Lily. And this is why it's so important for you to listen and to stay here until we can be sure it's safe for you. Do you understand?"

"Yeah." For the first time since the serious conversations had started in this bunker, Romeo laid his open hand on the cushions between them. She caught it and squeezed it so hard, he sucked a breath in through his teeth. Still, he didn't look away from the man they both hoped would finally give them some real answers.

"Let me start by saying that I'm sure you won't like a good deal of what I'm about to say." Ozias took a long drink of his own tea to wash the food down, and while it looked like a casual, careless thing to do, she saw quite clearly that he was trying not to lose his nerve. "If your mother is the witch who's caused the Black Heron Society such grief over the last few months, then yes, I saw her. Yes, she's alive, but she's been mistreated, Lily. How much, I can't say, but it was enough that I can say it with certainty. At least physically."

"I know." She nodded.

"I'll also say that when I saw her, she was smiling."

She barked a laugh and had to put the clay cup on the table to keep from spilling it. Romeo and Ozias both stared at her like she'd lost her mind. "Sorry." She cleared her throat. "Sorry. I only...yeah, I knew that already too." She smirked at her companion and nodded. "She's been giving them hell."

"It seemed that way, yes." The old man pulled quickly on his beard. "And the society members who had to handle her weren't happy about it at all. Which is why they came to me."

"What?" It was a good thing she'd set the cup down. Otherwise, she would have thrown it at him. "You helped those twisted people?"

Her friend squeezed her hand and whispered, "It's okay."

"It's not okay. I'm not gonna sit here and have a nice chat with anyone who helped my mom stay one of their prisoners."

"I'm not proud of it," Ozias said quickly.

"You definitely shouldn't be."

"But I did what I had to do to protect my people and Otiylo. This entire region of Greece, Lily. And I did not help them. I merely chose to look the other way while they passed through my village."

She jerked her hand out of Romeo's and shoved both of them under her folded legs on the cushions. *Or I'm gonna blast this guy to bits.* "You can't say, 'I only did nothing' and expect that to be enough."

"I don't. I told you that you wouldn't like what you heard. But it was enough for my people and, all things considered, my country."

"So how much did they pay you?" The young witch narrowed her eyes at the man who'd failed to stand up for any of the magicals the Black Heron had abducted. His cowardice had effectively left them all to be tortured and drained of their magic and used for who knew what else.

"We made a deal, but there wasn't any money involved." Ozias stroked his beard again, which seemed to be a nervous habit. "The few magicals assigned as your mother's handlers have taken her from place to place, mainly in the hopes that she'll give them what they've taken from everyone else."

"Yeah, I know that too. We've followed them."

The man's eyes widened. "You must be very good at what you do."

"I had a good teacher." She didn't even blink as she held the man in her burning glare. "And you let them take her."

"My pact with the Black Heron was simple, Lily. It's only been a few months, but Otiylo is now one of the safest places in the world because of it."

"Obviously not. We were attacked in your town."

"And, most likely, that's because of what you brought with you."

Yeah, he said he knew about the coin. I hope the man isn't about to repeat his daughter's accusations. "Before me, then. Before I disturbed the peace. Why is this town so safe?"

"I agreed to let the Black Heron pass through here as needed, without interference from me and mine and without resistance. And in return, they agreed to leave my people alone—no kidnappings, no murders, and no...experiments."

Lily rolled her eyes. "This is unbelievable. You actually trust them to keep their word?"

"Not at all. But a blood pact takes care of the trust factor." He leaned forward over the table between them. "I did what I had to do to keep my people safe. And I had no choice in the matter when they brought your mother through Otiylo. Even if I'd known how close you were or what she can do—what you can do, Lily—I wouldn't have been able to act against the pact I made. I hope you can understand that."

With flaring nostrils, she took a deep breath and exhaled slowly. "So why are all your magicals hiding out underground?"

"We still have to keep things relatively hidden. You know this. Most of the town is comprised of witches, yes. We have a few werewolves and a few fairies come through every now and then. But there are still non-magicals above us, and we didn't want to bring them into this any more than they already are simply by living here."

Romeo cleared his throat. "Yeah, we definitely noticed the creepy, abandoned-town vibes. Don't they think it's a little weird too?"

"Probably. There's not much we can do about that, and it's up to them whether or not they want to stay. Most of them have been here for generations. Maybe, when things are safer for all of us in the future—although I can't say with any certainty that it will happen—maybe our neighbors will come to understand what we've done here and how we've kept them safe from people like the Black Heron too. Until then, yes. Most of our magicals are belowground now. It's easier for us that way."

"Of course it's easier to hide." She shook her head. "That doesn't mean it's the best choice."

"You and I agree completely on that, Lily. But we're not hiding. That scrying pool"—Ozias gestured toward the giant marble basin in the center of the room—"connects to five others throughout Greece. One in Albania and one in North Macedonia as well. We're doing what we can, with what little power we have, to make sure that those magicals we can reach are kept safe as well."

The werewolf was intrigued. "You're fighting for them."

"In the ways we can, yes. Greece is protected from the chaos, which I'm sure you've noticed on your travels. The Black Heron has a wide reach."

"We definitely noticed." Lily wouldn't easily forget the people they'd met between Charleston and Greece—all those they'd helped, those who'd helped them, and a few they hadn't been quick enough to protect, too. "Ozias, I'd really like to get to the part where that...pact you made has anything to do with me. Besides you offering a safe place for those people to hold my mom prisoner even longer before they moved off to wherever they're going next."

"It has quite a fair amount to do with you, Lily. I can't expect you to know this. Very few people do, and all of them, of course, are Greek." The man cracked a small, wry smile. "You've seen the carvings of the Olympian gods on the scrying pool. If my daughter came to your aid above-ground like she said, I assume you've also seen the weapon our family has used for centuries."

"That trident's a family heirloom?" She fought hard not to laugh. *None of this is funny. That's what makes it so hard.*

"The spell behind it, yes. The Anagnos have been here for a very long time and we've always had a very good relationship with the Oracles."

"Like the Oracle of Delphi?" Romeo asked and folded his arms.

She shot him a sideways glance. "It sounds like someone paid attention in high school English class."

"What? Those are cool stories."

"To be clear, those are stories." Ozias took a deep breath and lowered his shoulders like he'd be relieved of a heavy burden in simply telling them what came next. "But the Oracles are real and they've talked about you, Lily."

SIXTEEN

"I'm not exactly sure that's a good thing." Lily retrieved her cup of lukewarm tea and took a long sip, merely for something to do.

Ozias regarded her with a searching look. "Whether it's good or bad doesn't quite apply as far as the Oracles are concerned. They see what they see and they tell those of us who still listen."

"So Greece has its own private version of storytellers, huh?"

"No, the two are very different. Although I see how you'd draw the connection. The Oracles see the past and present. They draw them into a single thread. They can touch you once and know everything there is to know about you, including what to reveal and what to set aside. They read magical history like a book, only forward and backward at the same time. There may be a few other directions I haven't noticed yet, too. Storytellers, I believe, are the keepers of magic itself, are they not? They feed the force that makes us who we are but use it to craft their tales. Of course, if any of us had ever met a storyteller in person, maybe we'd have a better chance at comparing notes."

The couple exchanged a knowing glance, and Romeo shrugged and gave her the floor one more time. She looked at the old man and smiled. *He's trying. I'm still gonna enjoy this.* "We have met a storyteller. A whole tribe of them, actually. It was small, but they happened to be in New Mexico while we were passing through."

He cleared his throat. "You...you've seen..." He shook his head and made no effort to hide his surprise. "Did you speak to him? See him perform? How does that work?"

"She had at least twenty years on you if I had to guess." She nodded. "And when she spoke—at least when she told her stories—she moved like she was our age." She gestured at her friend and herself, and he chuckled quietly. "We did talk to her a few times and I'll simply say that storytellers can definitely see the future too."

The werewolf scratched his eyebrow and frowned as he immediately remembered Amal's words of warning mere days before that warning went into effect when a group of Black Heron werewolves strung him up in chains. "Yeah. Definitely."

"Well that's...hmm." Ozias looked at his guests, clearly nonplussed, then broke into a wide grin. It looked incredibly odd surrounded by all that gray beard when he hadn't really smiled at them at all yet. "Maybe, if you feel like humoring an old witch, you'd be willing to tell me a few more things about this storyteller you met. I honestly wasn't sure I believed they existed until now."

"You said we'll have to stay down here for a few days, didn't you?" She shrugged. "I guess we'll need all we can find to pass the time without losing our minds."

He nodded. "It gets easier the more you do it."

"It might be easier if you told us what these Oracles have said about me, specifically." *I'm honestly a little fed up with the circular conversation here.*

"Yes. Of course." The old man bowed his head, closed his eyes, and searched for the words to tell them what needed to be said. "The Oracles have been watching you, Lily. Not for long but long enough to know what you are."

"I already know what I am."

"Most of it, probably. A storyteller read part of your future, I assume. You may have seen other visions of the same."

"I told Cosima all this and she didn't believe me." Lily glanced across the large room but couldn't find the old man's daughter or her thick black braid. *She probably went through one of those secret doors. It wouldn't surprise me if there are more than one.*

Ozias sighed. "Cosima...takes her responsibilities very seriously. I won't apologize for her decisions, but I am sorry for the added frustration it's caused you."

"That's fine. I know what I saw and I knew my mom was here. So did you."

"Yes, and you saw your mother through one of the Black Heron's relics, didn't you?" The man regarded her with real interest, and where his daughter had shown fear and suspicion, he was completely open to whatever Lily's answer might be.

"The most recent time? Yeah." She nodded. "That's how I saw her."

He rubbed his mouth. "Lily, anyone inducted into the Black Heron Society—if one could even call it an induction—goes through a...well, it's a nasty process. It's far worse than invoking a blood pact. I've seen it done here." He raised his hand to stop her when she opened her mouth to protest. "All those magicals were completely willing. Let me make that clear. And the system they've set up for communicating with each other is accessible only by those who have been through that initiation."

She rolled her eyes. "Again, I'm not part of the Black—"

"Until you."

"What?"

Ozias nodded and took a sip of his own tepid tea. "I don't doubt that there are others in the world like you, Lily, although you're very rare. Three Oracles I've visited have said the same thing, and I've learned to trust their wisdom during my lifetime. Do you know what an Optatus is?"

"Um...no." She frowned and wondered why the word sounded so familiar but didn't bring up instant recognition. "Do you?"

The man smirked and nodded. "It's a very old word for a very old line of witches—much like the storytellers and the Oracles and like the generations of my family who have protected and used the type of spells we pass down through our family line. Yours is even more in the blood if we're pointing out the differences. Optatus can be literally translated to 'desire.'"

Lily scoffed. "Succubi may or may not actually exist, Ozias, but I'm definitely not one of those."

"No. You are definitely a witch. An Optatus. That means that the core of your magic—the thing that makes you so different from ninety-nine percent of the world's witches—responds to what you desire, Lily." He raised his eyebrows and waited for the revelation to sink in.

"That doesn't make any sense." With a glance at Romeo, she shook her head. "If my magic gave me what I wanted, I wouldn't have spent the last few months tracking my mom. We'd be home already."

Ozias' lips twitched into a restrained smile. "I don't think it works like that."

"So how does it work?" Lily swallowed and for the first time, forced herself to really pay attention to what the man was saying. *If this is real, he might actually tell me what I need to know about my black-cloud spell. Maybe even exactly how to get Mom out of there...once we find her. Again.*

"Correct me if I'm wrong, but I imagine you're incredibly skilled with puzzles of one kind or another."

"Again, that came from having a really good teacher. My mom taught me everything I know."

"Perhaps she doesn't even know this about herself, then."

"What do you mean?"

"An Optatus witch does not appear out of nowhere like a storyteller, Lily. Not even like an Oracle. Like I said, it's in the blood. So whether or not your mother was aware of what the two of you really are, she is most definitely an Optatus herself."

When she looked at Romeo again, she found him staring at the mostly untouched plate of food, his eyebrows raised as he thought through some obviously astounding things and kept them to himself. "I'm reasonably sure she doesn't desire to still be the Black Heron's prisoner..." she began, her frown indicative of her own thought processes.

"But she was the one who taught you how to utilize the skills you were born with. To use them practically, correct? You've always managed to find the answer to any problem, haven't you? Even when the odds are stacked against you. Whatever you're looking for, if you want to find it badly enough, you do. Whenever you set your mind to something, you reach that goal, no matter who or what is put in your way to keep you from it."

"The guy pinned you down perfectly, Lil." Romeo looked at her and worried at the inside of his cheek.

"But that's—" She laughed. "That's the description of any person who works hard at anything they want to do. It doesn't make me a rare breed of witch."

"But the Black Heron's relic does."

"The coin?" Lily frowned.

"This is how being an Optatus works, Lily." Ozias spread his arms wide. "You had this coin, however it came into your possession. You knew that activating it would help you find your mother. I hope you knew of the consequences before you decided to use it." She nodded slowly. "Then it was worth it to you. You are not a part of that society and are not easy prey for them and their plans. You are an Optatus. You wanted to activate that coin to find your mother, and whatever you did to make that happen doesn't truly matter. The fact is that you accomplished your goal because it was what you desired. Honestly, I can't say there is any other explanation for it."

"Lily..." Romeo leaned toward her, his eyes wide with a mix of awe, confusion, and a little excitement. "Your shadow-bird."

"But that's only... I thought it was the black cloud—"

"What black cloud?" he swallowed and leaned forward, more captivated by this than by hearing they'd met a storyteller.

"It's a spell." She swiped the hair away from her face and glanced at the low ceiling above them. "I used it once months ago in Canada. I had no idea what it was, but it helped us—well, it got us out of trouble." Romeo smirked. "But that was a complete accident. Whenever I tried to use it before, it was either interrupted or I simply...couldn't."

"Except for two nights ago on the beach," Romeo muttered.

"Yeah, and that made the shadow-bird."

"And you said that's what activated the coin—"

"Show me," Ozias cut in to interrupt their side conversation in hushed voices.

Lily blinked. "That's probably not a good idea."

"You'll be fine, Lily."

The werewolf leaned forward. "No, she means it's not a good idea for you. And maybe everyone else in here."

"If Lily wanted to hurt me and everyone else in this

compound, then yes, I'd agree with you. But that's not what you want, is it?" The old man settled his gaze on Lily and raised his eyebrows.

Maybe at the beginning of this conversation... She shook her head. "No. That's not what I want."

"Then I have every confidence you'll contain this spell and use it in the safest way possible for a demonstration. I want to see it."

She looked from Romeo to Ozias and back again and found herself the odd one out in this decision. Even Romeo thought she should do what the trident-wielding friend of the Oracles had asked. "This is crazy," she muttered and shook her head. But she raised her hands anyway and prepared to conjure the one spell she hadn't properly mastered. *I don't even know what it's supposed to do.* "What if I can't stop it?"

"Have you tried?"

"Well, yeah—"

"Then you'll try again and you'll succeed." The bearded witch nodded and leaned back on the cushions, held his knees, and rounded his back for a short stretch. "Go ahead."

Lily puffed a sigh and focused on her hands. She clapped them and summoned the black cloud in the only way she'd learned how—by thinking about it. When she drew her palms apart, there it was—the dark, flashing spark of a pitch-black spell. It churned between her hands and grew with every inch she spread farther and farther apart. It was easier to control her arms and her muscles now after all the time she'd practiced like this in Romania. *Except it's not the same. I was trying to activate the heron coin on that beach. This guy only wants me to show off.*

Her arms shook after only a few seconds, and she glanced up from her spell and saw his face. His wide eyes were fixed on the roiling, rumbling cloud between her hands. The illumination it gave off seemed the opposite of light—like she'd cast a shadow over his face instead. The thin streaks crackled through the darkness she'd summoned like lightning in a tiny storm. An ear-splitting crack burst from her spell and echoed fiercely in the bunker. Ozias startled and quickly shook his head. "That's enough."

She swallowed thickly and glanced at the black cloud. It pushed against her hands as if it tried to grow and desired to be let loose. "I..." She forced her hands together and her muscles strained to direct all that power back where it came from—inside her.

"I've seen what I needed to see," Ozias added and continued to stare at the dark, swirling force between her hands. "Recall it."

"I'm trying." Her shoulders and biceps burned with the tension of trying to shove all that magic back into a manageable size.

"Now, Lily!" The old man's voice boomed almost as loudly as her spell had.

The young Optatus witch shouted under the strain and the agony in her arms and shoulders. Then, in a single instant, she clapped her hands with a little puff of black smoke and the cloud was gone.

She closed her eyes and exhaled a heavy sigh. "I told

you that was a bad idea." The bunker was so quiet, she heard the hollow echo of her own words bounce back at her. For a few seconds, she thought Ozias would kick her out.

Finally, he sniffed and nodded slowly. "Good ideas are never good ideas if the bad ones don't exist. I'd say you did fine."

She wanted to believe him, but the unsettled glimmer in his eye made that hard to do.

SEVENTEEN

"There's no doubt in my mind." Ozias busied himself with pouring another round of tea for all of them, but the lack of steam in any of their drinks made him grimace. "I told you I'd have something stronger, didn't I?"

Romeo shrugged. "You might've mentioned it."

"I think now's the time for it. Excuse me." The old man stood from the cushions on the floor without any apparent trouble, nodded at his guests once more, and wound between his followers in the bunker. The other witches had already returned to whatever it was they'd been doing before their leader lost his cool, but Lily felt their stolen glances at her anyway.

"I shouldn't have done that." She stared at the table, the untouched food, and the cold tea. "That was reckless."

"Not when it's an Optatus doing all the heavy lifting." Romeo was already studying her face by the time she looked at him, and he wore the only genuine smile right now in the underground hideout for rebel Greek witches.

That's probably the best way to describe them. She shook her head. "How do we even know any of that Optatus stuff is real?"

"We don't, not really. But it makes more sense than anything I've heard in the last few days. Maybe since we found Darius and he told us what the Black Heron's really up to." He caught her hands and turned them over to inspect her palms before he chuckled. "You're packin' some serious heat in those hands, Lil."

She rolled her eyes. "I don't know if it's the right time to joke about this. There probably isn't a right time at all with that spell. It's not...seriously, it's not funny."

"Okay. But you're making the same face right now that you made when our parents caught us in the treehouse."

"What?" She chuckled but even that was hard to keep to an appropriate level. "I can't believe you remember that."

"I remember it because it was hilarious—that face you're making right now. When you know what someone thinks of you and you know it's not true."

"Our parents thinking that we were fooling around in the treehouse isn't really on the same level as Ozias thinking I'm some dark-magic monster who shouldn't be let out of this bunker maybe ever."

"But you still think it's funny."

"I don't—" A snort escaped her, and she had to look away from him to keep from cracking up completely. "Okay, it's only funny because he wanted to see it so badly. And... Maybe he crapped his pants."

The werewolf didn't have any problem throwing his head back and laughing the way she wanted to. It echoed through the room and earned them many odd looks, especially so soon after she had terrified everyone with her black-cloud spell. A few muffled bursts of her own laughter escaped before she bit it down and slapped his arm playfully.

"Sorry." He covered his mouth, leaned away from her, and closed his eyes until he could get himself back under control. When he looked at her again, his smile was contained but sincere. "If we can't laugh about this now, Lil, we're in serious trouble."

"Yeah." She took one more glance around the room of witches, all of them waiting for Ozias to tell them what to do with their odd new guests. "We might be in trouble anyway."

"Hey, I didn't do anything."

She jabbed her elbow into his ribs, and he chuckled before he draped his arm around her. "You told me to do it."

"Lily, if anyone can claim peer pressure as an actual excuse, it's not you."

"Yeah, okay."

They sat on the cushions like that for a few minutes and simply watched the witches, who watched them in turn. Ozias finally reappeared from wherever he'd gone and held a large bottle in one hand and three small, shot-sized glasses in the other. He puffed out a sigh as he sat on the cushions around the table and set everything down gently. "We might spend most of our time underground these days," he said with a bright smile, "but that doesn't mean we don't know how to make the best of it."

"That does tend to make things better." Romeo nodded, his smile growing until he realized he had no idea what was in that bottle. "That is booze, right?"

"Hmm? Oh." The man chuckled. "Yes. Absolutely. This is tsipouro. Actually, there's an older couple who live on the row closest to the cliffs. Maybe you saw them on your way through. They've distilled this stuff for as long as I've known them. I could have all the magic in the world and still not make a batch of tsipouro as perfect as the Galanos do." He uncorked the bottle, inclined it toward the glasses, and paused. "I'm sorry. That was...distasteful of me."

"You mean talking about what you'd do with all the magic in the world?" She smiled sweetly at him, although they all thought the same thing. *Because that's exactly what the Black Heron's trying to do with their giant, stolen-magic spell. I really can't help feeling a little bad for the guy right now.*

Ozias cleared his throat. "Yes. I'm...still trying to wrap my head around the fact that it's what we're facing right now. Whether it's the immediate future—which I sincerely hope isn't the case—or somewhere farther down the road than I'll be walking in this life." Finally, he poured each of them a small but very full glass of the tsipouro and stood the bottle on the table.

"When we finally catch up with them," Lily said and nodded before she'd even touched her glass, "I'll do everything I can to make sure that doesn't happen in any future."

The man looked at her with wide eyes as if she'd said the most insulting thing possible. "You know, I would have told anyone else that it was a foolish thing to say and an impossible thing to do. It actually sounds like hope when an Optatus says it."

"We have more than enough of that to go around." Romeo raised his glass. "I, uh...I'm not sure what the right toast is for a secret hideout full of Greek witches."

"To us." Ozias nodded, and the couple repeated it after him.

I bet that sounds distinctly different without the translator spell.

Three full glasses clicked briefly and they drank.

Lily didn't stop to see whether the men sipped or threw the whole thing back like a shot. She chose the latter and almost laughed when she saw they'd done the same.

"You know, Romeo, I'm impressed by how well you're handling yourself down here." Ozias nodded and filled their glasses again.

"Um..." He glanced at Lily and frowned, his confusion showing most clearly in his flickering smile that wouldn't quite stay. "I'm not sure what you mean by that."

"Oh, uh...only that, as a werewolf, you seem rather unaffected by all this."

"All what?"

"So many witches. A secret hideout full of them, as you said." The man shrugged and glanced quickly from the werewolf to the young witch beside him. "Again, I'm not trying to offend either of you."

"Okay." Lily nudged Romeo and nodded. "Give the man a break."

"Thank you for the compliment." He nodded at their host and lifted his second glass of tsipouro. There wasn't a toast this time.

"It might help if you knew what actually happens with werewolves and magic." This time, Lily sipped her drink and studied the old man over the rim of her tiny cup.

"If it's different than what I've seen with my own eyes, please enlighten me."

"It's an allergy." She smirked.

"Come again?"

"Like hay fever. Or the seasonal sniffles."

Romeo snorted. "Yeah, that's it."

Ozias turned his head slightly and squinted. "Allergies?"

"With an actual treatment, too." She couldn't help herself this time and grinned before she downed the rest of the spirits.

"Oh..." Romeo sucked a breath in through clenched teeth and nodded. "Which I only might have enough of for the next...oh, fifteen to eighteen hours. Unless you wanna tell all your people to not use any magic at all for any period of time while we're down here. How long do we have to stay down here?"

The older man shook his head at him. "You don't, technically."

"Because I'm a werewolf?"

"Because you're not Lily."

"Right." Another sly smile crept over onto his mouth. "That makes sense."

"I am interested in this treatment, though. What is it?"

"Uh...it's kinda one of those powerful secrets you only share with someone when you're absolutely sure they'll use it for good." The werewolf lifted his glass and Lily snorted.

"That's fair. What if I told you we have a number of your kind in our community already who would love to hear what you've found. Do you think they'd use it for good?"

The slightly larger than average gulp Romeo had taken from the tsipouro stuck a little in his throat and the ensuing burn made him wheeze a cough. "You have—" He cleared his throat. "You have other werewolves down here?"

"In another room of our compound, for obvious reasons." Ozias nodded and topped off Romeo's almost empty glass. "But yes. You two aren't the only ones who've formed new friendships under the Black Heron's impending threat."

"We were friends before we were old enough to understand what that sentence means." Lily raised her eyebrows and shrugged. "But it doesn't really matter why it happened as long as the friendships are there."

"Lily..."

"Yeah, I know. Go for it."

Romeo gaped. "Seriously? Even if you..."

"Totally."

Chuckling, the old man poured himself another drink

as well. "It's amazing that you two understand each other at all with so many unfinished sentences."

"I guess that's simply how we work." She stared at the man until he noticed he hadn't refilled her drink yet either, and with a little jerk, he moved immediately to correct that oversight. *I should probably stop at this one if the stuff tastes better the more I drink it.*

"Can I see them?" the werewolf asked.

"Who?" Ozias blinked a few times, then realized what he'd missed and laughed. "Oh, yes. Yes, of course. I'll send someone to see if any of them are in."

"Do they go out a lot?" His eyes lit up even more at the thought of being able to run with a few wolves who weren't completely insane or trying to drug him into a werewolf fighting ring in the middle of the desert.

"As much as they can, when they're not...well, you know. Fighting with us."

He released a low whistle and shook his head. "Yeah, if anyone's in, definitely let me know."

"I'll ask as soon as we're finished here. Which—" The old man hiccupped and grunted. "We might be anyway, hmm?"

"I have a few more questions." Lily raised a finger in the air and talked over her thick-feeling tongue. *Maybe I should've stopped at two drinks.* "The warlocks and that other guy... They attacked us up there even with your blood-pact thing. What's to stop any more of them from... from coming down here for us?"

"Oh, hmm. Yes. They will try to come for you, I think, if they know you're here." Ozias looked at her from beneath heavy lids. "We have wards all around us. And, of course, no one knows the way in or out except those loyal to our—" He released something between another hiccup and a small belch and patted his chest. "Our cause and Otiylo, of course."

Romeo glanced at Lily and the old man, both of whom seemed to have become surprisingly drunk in such a short amount of time. He smirked. "Teleporting isn't the only way?"

Ozias shook his head. "It's merely the fastest. So as of now, no one knows you're there. I mean here. After a few more days, they won't even know if you're still in Otiylo or gone on somewhere else."

"When I use the heron...the co—the heron coin." Lily shook her head in an effort to clear it. "They can track me after that. That's what the Och—the Ochooli—" She sighed. "The gypsies told me that."

"Never argue with them if you want to get something out of it, huh?" The old man chuckled at his own confusing joke. "Yes, the Black Heron can track you. They have been already. But it doesn't last very long in the bigger scheme of things—perhaps a few days. When did you...use the relic last?"

She hummed and tried to count backward through the last few days. "I'm not sure. This tsipouro is really strong."

"You're welcome." The bearded man bobbed his head. "Oh, I...I told you the Galanos make theirs twice as strong as most, didn't I?"

Romeo burst out laughing. He felt a little buzz but

nothing near what the other two were going through right now. "You skipped that part."

Ozias squinted at him, a broad grin appeared above his graying beard, and he joined him in another round of laughter. The man leaned so far forward over the low table, Lily thought he would fall face-forward onto it and pass out right there.

"I wasn't trying to drunk this much—" She frowned at her own words, and when Ozias pointed at her with another bark of laughter, she couldn't help but give in to it. *We'll stay down here for a while, anyway. It's not like I have to get up early and go anywhere.* Romeo scratched the back of his head as he laughed, and she stuck her tongue out at him. "Well, thank you, Galanos family."

"To us!"

EIGHTEEN

L ily definitely didn't have to get up early for anything the next morning, but she wasn't the only one who spent the night in the bunker full of rebel witches. Whether or not the others had drunk as much as she had—which really wasn't much, all things considered—most of them were up before she'd had enough time to completely sleep it off.

"Yeah, toss it over there," a man shouted, followed by a clattering thump of what sounded like a collection of falling books.

With a groan, she pushed up from the cushions and scowled at the light of the glowing, magical spheres below the ceiling. *I literally can't remember if I willingly chose to sleep here or simply passed out. That's not a good start.* Then she noticed that Ozias wasn't anywhere near the scene of their drinking and neither was Romeo.

She rubbed the stiffness out of her neck and searched the huge room underground, her vision a little blurry and her head spinning. There were fewer witches than the night before, but it still took her a while to zero in on Romeo heading her way from across the room. "Oh, my God." She groaned and rubbed her throbbing temples. "He's almost bouncing."

"Morning." He grinned when he reached the cushions, carrying a massive plate of food she didn't want to think about looking at. "How are you feelin'?"

"Probably far worse than I look."

He sucked a hesitant breath in through his teeth. "I dunno, Lil. You're lookin' rough, to be honest."

She glared at him long enough to make him laugh. "You're supposed to be the voice of encouragement, aren't you?"

"Oh, I am?" He sat on the other side of the low table, set the heaped plate on it, and extended a fork toward her. When she made no effort to take it, he finally put it down so he could focus on eating. "I guess I missed the part where we agreed on that. Honestly, I think watching you and Ozias drink together last night was the closest thing I'll ever get to what it's like watching a werewolf in a room full of spellcasting." He loaded his fork and chuckled. "It's definitely fun to watch."

"I'm so glad you had such a good time. You don't happen to have any—"

"Yep." He slipped a bottle of water out of his back pocket and handed it over the table.

"Thank you. Did you go back to the Winnie?" It took her three attempts before she managed to open the top and she drank as much as her stomach would handle.

"Nope. These people are actually very prepared down here. It's kind of a weird combo of rebel witches and preppers all rolled into one."

"Now they only need to add a hangover cure, and they're all set."

Romeo shrugged. "Yeah. I talked to someone who knows someone who can get you a potion for that." He shoved a huge forkful of food into his mouth and grinned when she stared at him.

"I really hope you're not messing with me right now."

"Really, Lil? I think you already messed with yourself enough. Now that I think about it, I've never seen you hungover before. Or that drunk."

She nodded and chugged more water. "I wasn't planning on it. Although it wasn't as bad as a few nights in high school, though."

He snorted and choked a little on his breakfast. "High school?"

"We don't need to talk about it."

"Oh, I have ways of making you talk." Romeo leaned across the table and waved the next forkful of Greek breakfast food under her nose.

It took everything she had left not to smack the fork out of his hand. The thought vanished quickly, and she stopped and gazed wistfully at the plate of food. *He'll probably eat all that by himself if I don't say something.* "You were planning on sharing some of that, right?"

"Hence the extra fork. You probably won't need that for the gyro, though. That might be your best option right now."

"Oh, boy." With a long sigh, she forced herself to pick up the warm pita stuffed with lamb and yogurt and cucumber that she hoped would help settle her stomach. "You really know how to treat a hungover witch to a good time."

"I try."

It wasn't surprising that a little food and considerably more water made her feel better. *At least I can turn my head without being sick.*

Romeo, of course, finished the plate off in record time, propped himself against all the cushions, and sighed. "I know I already asked you this, but I thought I should probably double-check now that you're a little more sober."

"Barely." Despite herself, Lily chuckled.

"You really don't mind if I end up doing something with the other werewolves Ozias said were here?"

"Why would I?"

He shrugged. "I'm only making sure. I think...well, it's been a long time since I've done anything with other wolves. Even my dad."

"Yeah, Romeo, you don't have to ask for my permission about anything. You know that, right?"

"I know. That doesn't mean I don't wanna make sure you're okay if I step out for a few hours." He shifted sideways on the cushions and propped his head up in one hand. "Seeing as it's basically the only smart choice to stay here until the heron coin's...tracer or whatever disappears.

After that, we'll head out. I merely don't want you to think that I don't care about leaving you here."

She smiled and shook the hair out of her eyes. "It's not like I'd be much fun running around with a group of wolves in the middle of the night."

"I dunno, Lil. I bet you could find a spell that makes you extra fast if you really wanted to."

"No, thanks. I think I might actually let myself chill out for another day." She shrugged. "It's not exactly by choice, right? I honestly don't know if Ozias would let me out of here even if I begged. That would probably bring more society members to their front door again. And I'm sure Cosima would try to lock me up if I even suggested stepping out before they say it's safe."

"Yeah, she's a little...militant, isn't she?"

"This whole thing is, in a weird way."

"True."

They stared at each other for a few seconds before she lowered herself slowly onto the cushions again. "Thanks for bringing me breakfast."

"No problem. It's kinda my thing."

She rolled her eyes and smiled. "I think I might try to go back to sleep."

"Do you mind if I join you?"

"Definitely not."

It took a little shuffling around of numerous cushions before they had something remotely comfortable for both of them together. Finally, he lay behind her and settled his arm gently over her waist. "Hey, was last night our first real night not in the Winnie?"

Her eyes fluttered closed. "Wow. Actually, I think it was."

"Is it weird that I miss it already?"

Lily took his hand and laced their fingers. "Nope. I probably would have slept much better if we'd been able to go back." She began to slide off into sleep again and was barely awake enough to ask, "How come you didn't pass out like I did?"

"For all the headaches, Lil, being a werewolf has its perks. One of those is that it takes much more to make me pass out."

"Huh." She chuckled. "I think maybe last night is the only time I'd consider that a perk." He said something else after that, softly and with his lips brushing against her ear, but she was already in the place of slumber.

———

"LILY." Soft fingers brushed through her hair and made her smile sleepily. "Hey, Lil. Wake up. You're definitely gonna want to see this."

Romeo removed his hand and she almost shouted at him to put it back and keep up the mini head massage. Instead, she forced her eyes open and propped herself halfway up on the cushions. "What's going on?"

He helped her sit up and nodded toward the adjacent wall. "Check the kid out."

"What ki—oh."

A little boy of perhaps five or six sat against the wall with a collection of soft, smooth stones he must have collected from the beach. He was scrawny and shirtless, his skin as tanned as most of the other witches they'd seen in Otiylo. But his hair was a striking shade of bone-white. It didn't seem to bother him that he was the only child down there at all—or at least the only one they had seen so far. Instead, he was perfectly content with his rocks, which he'd laid out on the floor in a straight line. Then, slowly and with far more deliberation than she had seen in a child that age, he tapped the first stone.

It sparkled at his touch and shimmered in the light of the magical orbs above them before it began to move.

"Is he—"

"Shh. Watch." He settled his hand on her back and nodded. "He's done this for the last half-hour."

The stone didn't so much move as it changed its shape, rose up, and elongated as if it melted in reverse. In only a few seconds, the plain beach rock had transformed into a tiny gray horse with a mane and tail that waved in an unseen breeze. It stamped its hoof on the stone floor and shook its head.

The boy tapped each of the stones in turn and waited for the next to fully shift into a new shape before he turned his magic onto the next one. In fifteen minutes, he had a herd of a little under two dozen stone horses that pranced and snorted in front of him. A small, unselfconscious smile pulled at his lips before he began to talk to himself. His expressions grew more and more animated as he muttered something she couldn't hear. Despite that, she thought she knew what he was doing.

The more the boy said, the more the stone horses

moved. Slowly, he raised his hands and his eyes widened as his small smile spread into a grin. When he shook his hands, the horses burst into a gallop—proportionate to their tiny size—in a large circle in front of the young witch.

Lily laughed softly. "Do you think he's a storyteller?"

"Probably, yeah. There's the hair, plus being able to pull out a spell like that simply for fun?"

"That's incredible. I wonder if anyone else here has realized it yet."

"He turned those stones into fish, a pack of wolves, and butterflies. Those never got off the ground, but I guess rocks have a hard time flying. It's kinda hard not to notice, Lil."

She looked at him and raised her eyebrows. "Unless no one knows how to see a storyteller when he's sitting right under their feet."

"True."

The boy uttered a high-pitched giggle as the horses ran in their circular stampede. One of them broke from the others and headed directly toward the couple. It was almost trampled by two women who crossed the huge bunker, their arms laden with stacks of folded cloth.

"Castor," one woman said sternly and peered over her armful to flash him a warning glance, "you really need to keep your toys out of the way, all right? Someone will get hurt."

"Don't be too hard on him," her companion muttered. "What else is he supposed to do? The poor kid's all alone down here."

"He still needs to learn to pick up after himself, Hali. That's part of growing up."

"He's a long way from growing up..." The witches' voices faded into the bustle of all the others moving around the bunker and performing their duties.

Castor stared after them from his place on the ground. He didn't look all that angry or embarrassed, but he certainly didn't look particularly concerned about obeying them, either.

The stone horse that had escaped, having realized it wouldn't be crushed by any unsuspecting boots—for now— continued its course across the floor toward Lily and Romeo on the cushions. It reached them in a few more seconds, trotted to a halt, and reared on its hind legs. The mouth opened, although there was no sound.

She giggled in amazement and covered her mouth with a hand. "This is fantastic." When she looked at the boy, she found him staring at her with a mixture of curiosity and admiration. Even more striking was his one dark-brown eye and the other a piercing icy-blue. "Woah," she muttered. She smiled and raised a hand for a little wave. *Hopefully, this kid doesn't decide to start running from me too. Where would he go, anyway?*

The child studied them for a moment, then muttered something to his herd of stone horses. All his tiny creations changed course and hurtled across the floor toward the two visitors. The boy pushed to his feet and followed them.

NINETEEN

F or some reason she wasn't quite sure of, Lily felt a little nervous to be so close to the boy. *It's like seeing Amal and all her drummers in a tiny little body. All that power in a kid.*

Castor moved swiftly toward them. His skinny arms swung at his sides and his bare chest stuck out in careless pride. He continued to stare at her until he reached the edge of the cushions when he glanced briefly at the stone horses that pranced around his feet now that he'd joined them. He grinned at all the soundless whinnies from the spirited horses he'd brought to life with his magic and his stories. When his gaze lifted to meet hers again, his blue eye flashed with a bright light.

Unless I'm imagining things.

"Hi." The boy stuck his hand out and held it in front of her face.

"Hi. I'm Lily." She tried not to laugh as she raised her hand awkwardly high to take his. She lowered it to a comfortable level for them both and shook his hand. But as soon as their hands lowered together, he squeezed her fingers in a surprisingly tight grip. His eyelids fluttered rapidly for a few seconds and when he opened them again, there was no mistaking the flash of magic blooming inside him. That blue eye sparked and swirled, and the boy finally released her hand.

"You're the one they're talking about." There wasn't any fear there, only mild surprise as if he hadn't expected the stranger, or her companion, to be anything but another refugee taking shelter in Otiylo. Or, perhaps, coming to help fight for it.

"Who?" Lily's smile faded slightly. *I guess it's not weird that someone's talking about me in one way or another.*

"The voices. There are many voices from...the future, I think." His brows drew together as he tried to express the things he knew so well himself but hadn't yet learned how to articulate.

"Well, I hope they say good things about me, at least." Lily tucked her hair behind her ears.

"Not good or bad." Castor tilted his head and studied her face. Somehow, it looked far too much like Amal the storyteller, who'd studied people's faces with her hands and saw more in her blindness than most people saw in their lifetimes. "Things will change for everyone if you don't do what you're supposed to do—in the fire. Things will change for everyone if you do it anyway. That's up to you."

She glanced at Romeo, who seemed as discomforted by

the boy's apparent prophecy as she was. "Um..." She nodded. "Thanks for letting me know."

"They say that's what I'm supposed to do. I liked making these more." He stooped to pick up one of the stone horses, which pranced on his open palm as the only creature to have this type of special attention.

"Where did you learn to do that?" the werewolf asked and gestured at the magic beasts.

"Here."

"In this room?"

Castor shrugged. "And others. There isn't much to do down here, but I don't get bored. My mama brings me rocks, and I like to play with them, so..." He returned the horse to the floor with the others and focused on the newcomers with frank scrutiny. "You'll leave soon. I'm sorry that you're so sad."

"I'm not..." Lily smiled, startled by the genuine compassion coming from a kid this age. "I'm not sad. It's nice down here, but I think I'll be ready to leave when we do."

"Oh. Then you will be sad. Sometimes, I get sad when I'm confused." He shrugged again. "Do you wanna watch me make something else?"

"Sure." She glanced at Romeo, who nodded and echoed the sentiment.

"Okay. I have more. I'll get them." With a curt nod, the boy spun on his heels and raced across the busy underground compound, his bone-white hair flopping up and down on his head with each step.

"So it's hard enough to believe everything kids say

anyway." Lily turned to look at Romeo and finally straightened fully on the cushions. "But knowing he's a storyteller—"

"Are you sure of that?"

"You heard the kinds of things he said. Couldn't you feel it?"

He pursed his lips and frowned slightly. "I did. It felt exactly like talking to Amal."

"Exactly."

"Creepy."

She shook her head. "Well, he's a kid. I don't think he'd be able to tell me what he meant even if I asked."

"Like that part about you doing what you're supposed to do in the fire." He rubbed the back of his neck—something he only did when he was sheepish, uncertain, or discomforted. "Lily, I don't know if that's worth paying attention to. Kids have imaginations."

"Yeah, and most kid witches can't bring a whole slew of rocks to life and make them run around like living things." She pointed at the herd of stone horses, which had now slowed at the edge of the cushions to apparently graze on the dust-coated stone floor beneath them. "Rosalía was incredibly talented for her age. And she's definitely only a witch."

He snorted. "Only."

"I know, but when we compare witches to storytellers... Castor's not only a kid witch with incredible skills. He hears voices."

"You know, some people say that requires medication."

"Amal heard voices too. And she couldn't see much

more about me than the fact that I'd need that lapis lazuli stone to 'see in the dark.' I'm telling you, this kid is a storyteller."

Slowly, he ran his finger along the back of one of the stone horses. The thing spooked and bucked wildly with its hind legs. "Ow." He pulled his hand back, shook it, and frowned at her when she laughed. "Okay, he's definitely good at making these ridiculously lifelike."

"Magic is life." She raised an eyebrow. "That's what storytellers are for, isn't it?"

"Okay, I'm convinced. Hey, and for the record, I don't plan to do anything while we're here that's gonna make you sad."

She bumped her shoulder against his and shook her head. "It didn't even cross my mind. I wonder what that's gonna be, though. Maybe sad to say goodbye to probably the only kid storyteller we'll ever meet?"

He shrugged. "We won't find out until we get to the point where whatever we're told comes true."

"Yeah, I guess." *And why do I have the feeling that I'm gonna like whatever I'm supposed to do 'in the fire' far better than 'being so sad' when I leave?*

Bare feet slapped against the dusty floor again, and Castor returned carrying a backpack in his outstretched hand. It sagged at the bottom and looked heavy enough to make him fall over any minute if he took a wrong step. Finally, he slowed and approached his new friends on the cushions. Breathing heavily, he dropped the backpack with a thump and a few jumbled cracks. The stone horses darted away from the disturbance and circled each other and their creator until he sat on the floor in front of the couple and crossed his legs.

"Okay." He took a deep breath and grinned. "I brought them all. What do you wanna see?"

"Oh, that's a tough one." Romeo smirked. "Can you do werewolves?" Lily cast him a warning glance and he simply winked at her.

"Yeah, those are easy." The boy unzipped the backpack and thrust his hand inside to withdraw handful after tiny handful of the rocks his mom had apparently brought back for him while he'd been hiding down there for who knew how long.

"They're easy," she repeated and winked at Romeo. He rolled his eyes.

"Just one, though, 'cause I like other things." The boy looked at them with a tentative smile. "The other werewolves kept asking me to make the same thing too so it's a little boring. But I'll show you one."

She chuckled, and her companion tried to look serious when he nodded. "I appreciate you making an exception for me, bud."

"Castor," the boy corrected, stared at his pile of rocks, and searched for the one he wanted.

"Right. Castor. I'm Romeo."

"I know." Finally, the kid selected a medium-sized stone from the pile and held it up for his new friends to see. "All black, see?" They nodded. "Exactly like you sometimes, Romeo."

The werewolf almost choked on his surprise, and she stifled a giggle. "Yeah, sometimes," she said.

The only reaction the boy gave was to nod sagely like everything he'd suspected was falling into place the way it should. He set the stone on the ground away from the others and muttered something so softly, they couldn't even hear the words despite sitting so close to him this time. His finger touched the stone lightly, and it repeated the process the others had followed to morph and melt upward into its own shape—the shape he had commanded it to take.

When it was finished, a fully-clothed man stood in place of the stone and walked casually beside the pile of pillows as if he'd always been there and hadn't suddenly appeared. "He likes taking this shape," the boy said and his smile widened a little. "It makes him feel smart—like he can do anything he wants. He can think and speak and make people happy. But that's not all he is."

Lily looked away from the walking man made of stone and stared at Castor's face. *This is exactly the same as listening to Amal during the spirit walk. He's working his magic, all right. Telling a story.*

"The man sometimes likes to be something else. The other part of him is strong. It knows everything. Especially how to protect people the man loves." For a brief moment, he glanced at Lily and took her completely off guard. His blue eye flashed again, and the stone man morphed much quicker this time into a shaggy black wolf that was huge in proportion to the man's previous size.

"Oh, my God," she whispered and covered her mouth with her hand. When she glanced at Romeo, he stared at the miniature stone version of himself as a wolf and shook his head in complete bafflement.

"And this way," Castor continued, "when things go wrong, the wolf is there to do what needs to be done."

The stone wolf crouched and snarled soundlessly at some unseen enemy. Its muscles tensed—so clearly and strangely visible beneath the thick, rippling fur of black stone—before it pounced.

"Castor." The man who walked quickly toward them called the boy's name so loudly, it shattered his attention. It caught the couple's attention, too. All three of their heads whipped to look at the new arrival, who sounded incredibly angry. The magic wolf shrank into simply a stone in the middle of its leap and clattered on the floor. The horses shied away from it before they too fell back into the forms nature had given them.

When the man reached them, the boy sat within a ring of nothing but stones.

"I'm sorry," the newcomer said and stared at Lily with wide eyes.

Is he actually afraid of me? "Don't be sorry. We were only—"

"Castor, I don't know how many times I have to tell you to keep these games to yourself. No one's watching the ground for your animals. You'll hurt someone."

"They wanted to see," the boy replied softly and craned his neck to stare at the man. "They like it. And I only want to show someone what I can do."

The man licked his lips, his frown of anger melted into sadness, and he crouched in front of the boy. "I know. And

I'm so sorry that you don't have enough room to express yourself down here. But you know why Mama and I brought you here, don't you?"

"To be safe."

"That's right. I'm glad you were able to show these people, and I'm glad they liked it. But I think they might have a few more important things to do right now."

Castor shook his head. "They don't."

"We really don't," Lily echoed. *This poor kid.*

He looked past his son and met her gaze. "Well, thank you for giving him as much time as you have. Buddy, I want you to pick up all your rocks and take your bag to our room. Leave them there for the rest of the day, please."

"Da—"

"Castor. Do as I say."

The boy stared at him for a few seconds before he finally backed down and accepted his father's wishes. He didn't complain or make a face or try to argue further. Instead, he scooped all his rocks quietly into a pile and dumped handfuls into the backpack until they were all put away. He zipped it, took hold the handle, and stood. When he turned toward Lily and Romeo, he wore a tiny smile but it was only partly genuine. "It was nice to meet you."

"You too, Castor." Lily smiled in response.

"Thanks for the show," Romeo added.

He passed his father, who still crouched on the ground, and the man patted his son gently on the back before the kid lugged his bag through the throng of witches tending to whatever jobs were theirs today. With a sigh, the man ran a hand down his face and shook his head. "I really am sorry if he bothered you." His eyes begged Lily for forgiveness.

"Please don't be." She shook her head. "He's a really great kid. And he's incredibly talented."

"He didn't...say anything that was too...much, did he?"

"What?" She chuckled and shrugged. "There really isn't much anyone could say that's too much right now. He was completely fine."

"Okay. Well, thank you. It won't happen again." He actually bowed from where he crouched in front of the cushions. It seemed hard for him to stand, but before he could turn away, she stopped him.

"You know what he is, right?"

The man stopped and when he turned slowly toward them, he looked like he might burst into tears. "I assume you do too."

Lily nodded and Romeo gestured at the other side of the table. "Feel free to join us. If you're not too busy."

He took a halting breath and finally decided it was better to sit and talk it out than try to pretend he wasn't uncomfortable. With a nod, he stepped over the cushions and settled on the other side of the low table. "My name is Galen."

"I'm Lily."

"Romeo."

Galen nodded and closed his eyes to gather himself. "If you tell me my son's a storyteller, Lily, I'll know it's true."

She frowned. "Why does it matter what I tell you? You know your son better than I do."

"I saw what you did last night." He met her gaze,

glanced away in embarrassment, and finally managed to look at her for longer than two seconds. "The spell you cast. Castor's mother and I have seen that done only once before in our lifetimes, but the magic's unmistakable."

"Yeah, I definitely believe that." She nodded. "I... wasn't trying to scare anyone."

His chuckle sounded a little strained but he nodded. "Forgive me. I believe you, and it still doesn't change the way I feel. An Optatus brings more power with her than most of us in this place have combined. If your intentions were good, I'd still be terrified. I've seen an Optatus's intentions go from good to bad in the blink of an eye, and the bad is...very much that."

"Oh." She blinked. *So now I'm terrifying because of what I might be. It would've been nice for the Romani vision to show me that part.* "But it's not always set in stone. That an Optatus will always end up with bad intentions."

"Nothing is set in stone."

"Unless it's part of things a storyteller can see." Romeo glanced from the young witch to Castor's father, both of whom had thought the same thing already.

"Did he..." Galen covered his mouth with his hand and rubbed it in concern. "Did he tell you anything about yourself? About where things are headed for the rest of us?"

"Not in very much detail." She shrugged. "He said things would change for everyone whether I did what I was supposed to do or not. It doesn't really mean much."

The man nodded slowly, clearly disappointed. "Until the moment when it means everything."

They were silent for a few moments around the low

table. Lily had to ask, "How long has your son been down here?"

He winced at her words and frowned at the table. "A long time. It's coming up on a year, I think."

"But he goes up there sometimes, doesn't he?"

When the man looked at her, his eyes shimmered with tears. "He gets to play with the other children who come down here for a day or two before they're on their way again. And his mother brings him those...rocks." He sniffed but he didn't manage to hold back the first few tears so he wiped them away and pretended to ignore them. "She didn't want the storytellers to come for Castor so soon. He's only five and needs his parents. We brought him here to buy all three of us a little more time. And then, with everything that's happening up there...those dark-magicals..." He swallowed. "If they knew Castor was here—a storyteller with that kind of magic but no ability to protect himself—they'd come for him too. We don't have a choice right now, as it is."

He looks like he's about to be sick. Lily placed her hand on the table and leaned toward the man, hoping to catch his attention. Instead, he simply closed his eyes. "I am so sorry, Galen. You're doing what you have to do for your family. There's no shame in that."

"Thank you. Let's hope the Optatus does what she's supposed to do, then, huh? Maybe that'll change things enough for Castor to see the sky without worrying about who's coming from it for him." With that, the man pushed himself up from the cushions, nodded at them without looking at them, and stalked off across the wide room.

Her eyes swam with tears and she fought to swallow. Romeo's hand settled gently on her back and it almost made her cry. "I had no idea there was so much riding on this. On me."

"Hey, you can't say that it is, Lil. This seeing the future stuff is tricky."

She looked at him and studied his gaze. "I don't think it's tricky at all for the people who see it. Only for the rest of us." *Hold your breath, Lily. You can't fall apart now.* A few seconds of that seemed to do the trick and she wiped hastily at her eyes before any tears could fall. "I think I'll be really glad to get out of here."

"Yeah. I'm right there with you."

TWENTY

C astor had been a fun distraction from the tedium of sitting in a Greek witch bunker with absolutely nothing to do. Lily asked a few of the other witches if she could help with anything, but none of them had any extra chores. "Or maybe none for me," she muttered and watched the last group of strangers walk away from her after they too had told her to make herself at home and not worry about all the work.

Ozias found them again after lunch, smiling despite the dark circles under his eyes. "You look like you're doing well, all things considering."

"Excuse me?"

"After drinking." He shook his head and chuckled. "That's all I meant. I'm not nearly young enough to bounce back from last night, but you look like you're doing fine."

"Oh. Yeah, I am now." Lily turned toward the cushions, where Romeo had stretched out with his hand behind his head as if he actually enjoyed having absolutely nothing to do.

"And he looks quite...comfortable."

She laughed. "He does, doesn't he?"

"Do you think he might jump to life a little at the prospect of meeting with the others tonight?"

"The other werewolves?" When Ozias nodded, his gray beard billowing, Lily smirked. "Yeah, that'd probably put some pep in his step."

"That's good to hear. Would you like to tell him, or should I?"

She waved toward the lounging werewolf. "Be my guest."

Chuckling, the old man nodded at her and made his way toward the cushions and the low table. Romeo didn't move when the man approached but muttered something that made him laugh and shake his head. She grinned when, after a few seconds of the man delivering the news, her friend sat bolt upright from the cushions and grinned. Then, he leapt to his feet, slapped the man on the back as he shook his hand, and might as well have broken into a happy dance right there. When the man left him, he had to keep himself from running up to Lily.

He did, however, pick her up around the waist and squeeze her in his excitement.

"Woah, okay. Ow." She struggled to free her arms from his embrace and laughed.

"Sorry. I'm sorry. I only...sorry."

"You're really looking forward to it." She grinned at

him and brushed the dark curls away from his eyes gently. "I like seeing you this excited."

"I wish you could come."

"I know."

"He said..." Romeo glanced behind her at Ozias' retreating form. "He said we can leave in the morning."

"That fast, huh?"

"Yeah. So good news for both of us." He wiggled his eyebrows and bounced a little on his heels. "We'll be outta here. Done with the cabin fever."

"Right." *Except we still have to find out where they took my mom now, and I don't think we can do that without using the heron coin again.*

Exactly like he always did, Romeo could see on her face what she was thinking. "We'll find the way forward, Lil. After this, once we're back in the Winnie where we belong." She snorted. "I'm serious, though. We'll get away from these people to help them stay a little safer. And then, we'll decide what to do."

"Okay."

"Okay." He cupped her cheeks in both hands and kissed her fiercely. When he pulled away, she almost yanked him back toward her. "I really wish we weren't in a giant room with a whole group of other people right now."

"Woah, there." She laughed and wrapped her arms around his neck. "We can wait. And you have a night of wolfing around Greece to look forward to. We'll get to the other stuff when we're back on the road."

"Oh, the other stuff, huh?"

"Yeah." She bit her lip and he kissed her again to make his point.

"Okay, this is... I'm gonna be a little jumpy for the next few hours."

"When did Ozias say they'd meet you?"

"At ten." He shrugged. "He said he'd come to get me. I don't know how to tell time in this place."

Lily smirked and winked at him. "Probably with a watch."

"Hey, look at you. You're so smart."

"Not smart enough not to leave both our phones in the Winnie."

"Yeah, they probably don't even work down here." He hugged her tighter and glanced around the bunker. "And I'd simply stare at it while it counted down the minutes."

"We should probably find something to do, then. I can only handle you bouncing around like this for so long."

"Right. Right. I'll go find something."

He kissed her temple and released her to move quickly through the crowds of witches around them. None of these people looked at him the way they looked at her—with fear and uncertainty and a kind of respect brought by both of those things. *That's not the kinda respect I want. I bet this is how he feels in a room full of witches who don't like werewolves.*

The next group Romeo stopped to talk to seemed a little reluctant to accept whatever it was he said, but eventually, they agreed. After a series of pointing and nodding, he left the group and returned to Lily, who'd simply stood near the wall adjacent to the pile of cushions and watched the whole thing. "That was easy," he said. "Mostly."

"What was the hard part?"

"Convincing them that you actually did wanna help and were really good at almost anything."

She snorted. "They don't think I'm, like...incapable of doing anything but black-cloud spells, do they?"

"No." He glanced at the group of witches. Only one of them raised a hand and smiled. The couple returned the gesture. "I think they only want to let you do your own thing. I dunno. That maybe you wouldn't want to help."

"If I'm an Optatus witch, I don't really think that gives me any special privileges."

He shrugged. "Maybe only in Greece."

"Oh, boy. Okay. So what are we helping them with, then?"

Wiggling his eyebrows, Romeo spread his arms wide. "Sorting."

"Sorting what?"

"Food. Bottled water. Canned goods. Maybe herb jars, I think." He laughed at the confused frown she gave him. "I think they're bringing it all out here for us to kinda take over."

"They need help with sorting."

"That's what they said."

She grimaced. "I don't really think that's actually helping them, Romeo. I think that's their version of getting us out of the way."

"Huh. Maybe. Still, they were nice enough about it. And we have something to do for the next couple of hours.

It's better than me driving you nuts while I count down to ten o'clock."

"And better than me driving you nuts by having nothing to do."

"Okay!" He clapped his hands and spun in search of a suitable place to make their new workstation for their last night in Ozias's magical bunker. "Where should we do this"

Lily stared at him. *He's really geared up right now.* "I'm fine going back to the cushions."

"Oh. Oh, yeah. That sounds good. I guess we'll wait for our assignment, then."

She snorted. "I really hope you run your heart out tonight."

"Believe me, Lil." He flung his arm around her shoulders and pulled her toward him while he scanned the hideout for the group of witches who would finally give them something to do. "I will."

TWENTY-ONE

L ily had fallen asleep incredibly quickly after the almost five hours they'd spent sorting through what had to be literally everything Ozias's bunker had in supplies. She'd even eaten dinner, which surprised Romeo only in that she'd put away more than he had. "And that's what happens when a witch skips three meals in a row." He chuckled and stretched out on the cushions.

The bunker was incredibly quiet, most of the witches in Ozias's party having gone off to wherever it was they went at the end of the day. Soft snores rose beside him, and he turned his head to look at her sleeping on the pile of cushions. "We made it through today all right, didn't we?" Of course, she didn't answer but he smiled anyway, put his hands behind his head, and stared at the low ceiling. "And we'll make it through every other day, Lil. No problem." The silence grew even louder as he lay there, wide awake. "I wish I had a clock, though."

Right on cue, one of the hidden doors in the massive

room opened and slid back into the attached tunnels before it grated against the wall and clicked into place with an echoing boom. He sat up and quickly located the open door. A glance at Lily confirmed that she was, in fact, sleeping through all of it. "And you need it."

Ozias stepped out of the dark passageway on the other side of the room and strode toward them. His shoes whispered across the dusty floor, and he smiled at Romeo. "Time to get up and out."

"Excellent." With a grin, he rolled over and smoothed the blonde hair away from Lily's face and neck before he leaned down to whisper in her ear. "I'm going now." She hummed something unintelligible. "I'll be back before you know it 'cause you'll be asleep." He kissed her cheek and added, "I love you." She shifted a little in her sleep, and he caught the smile that flickered at the corners of her mouth. He pushed himself slowly from the cushions and headed toward Ozias.

The man nodded at the stacked pallets against the adjacent wall. "You've found ways to keep yourself busy, I see."

"Well, yeah. That was for both of us."

"Did it work for both of you?"

He turned to look over his shoulder for a final glance at Lily. "It worked for her. I'm still awake."

Ozias chuckled and shook his head. "Good. I'm sure you'll be as exhausted as she is once you come back in."

"I hope so."

They stepped through the open doorway and into the dark passage beyond. The old witch snapped his fingers, which made a silver spark, and the door rumbled shut behind them. In the complete darkness on the other side, he conjured a ball of light and floated it out of his hand to send it down the passage ahead of them. "You don't seem surprised by any of this."

Romeo uttered an airy chuckle. "I've traveled the world with a witch who's apparently an Optatus too. And she's been my best friend since I was six. There isn't much magic that surprises me anymore."

"Only best friends, huh?" The man cast him a sideways glance and tried to hold back a smirk.

"Well." He raised one shoulder in a careless shrug. "Probably a little more than that now." When the man chuckled again at that, he couldn't hide his grin even if he'd wanted to. "I gotta say, Ozias, this is the first time I've seen a whole group of witches all open to...you know...being friends with werewolves. Helping them, even. I get why they have their own space in your little underground kingdom—"

"Please." The old man shook his head, laughed, and waved him off with a dismissive hand. "It's not a kingdom. And we offered the werewolves their own space down here at the very beginning, not because we were afraid of spending more time with them. They deserve as much protection as the rest of us. So do you."

"Thanks." He nodded and tried to see ahead of them down the tunnel, but the floating orb of light only went so far. "That's what I'm saying, though. I haven't seen that very much. I know I'm not staying here or anything, but for what it's worth, I appreciate it."

"And I appreciate your acknowledgment. Things are changing, Romeo. Many things are going down dark roads, but there's still light at the end of a few tunnels." The man chuckled and pointed down the passage. "Like this one." They stopped at a nondescript part of the tunnel and Ozias snapped his fingers again with another flash of silver sparks. One more door shoved forward toward them and slid aside against the wall.

A soft orange glow spilled into the dark tunnel, and he stepped into the room first, followed by the visitor. "Sebastian," the man called.

Romeo looked across the room and realized that the orange glow was actually from fire—real torches mounted into the walls flickered in the slight draft out of the tunnels. *So no electricity down here and no magic for the werewolves without wolfsbane. This is some way to hang out underground.*

At the far end of the room—which was about half the size of the main bunker where he'd left Lily—six people lounged on a circle of armchairs and couches. Beside the circle was a dining table and chairs, and a few bookshelves lined the walls. A man in a brown turtleneck stood from the couch and left the others to approach them.

"It's good to see a new face." The man offered Romeo his hand and they shook. "I'm Sebastian."

"Romeo. It's good to be the new face. Thanks for letting me tag along."

"No problem. I remember what it was like when I first came down here. I wish I didn't." He chuckled. "I'm more than happy to take you out with us."

"Right."

"Ozias." Sebastian nodded at the old man, who returned the gesture and turned to leave.

"Show him the way back when you come in, will you? I'll sleep off the rest of this hangover." The door in the wall slid shut behind the old man, and Sebastian smirked.

"Hangover, huh?"

"I had nothing to do with it." He raised his hands in surrender and chuckled.

"No, I bet you didn't." Sebastian clapped him on the back and led him toward the circle of couches and armchairs. "All right. We have a number seven tonight, guys. This is Romeo."

"Hey." A few of the other werewolves raised their hands. They all nodded, and one woman with long, curly brown hair wearing incredibly tight jeans studied him avidly with a daring smile of approval. He merely nodded at them all and tried not to catch the woman staring at him.

"I'd introduce everyone, but really, none of us care at this point, right? Let's get outta here."

The five other werewolves lounging on the furniture stood together like someone had lit a fire beneath them all at once. One guy with spikey blond hair smacked Romeo on the back. "It's good to keep things interesting, right?"

"Real interesting." The woman with curly hair stepped beside him and batted her lashes. "I'm Alisha."

"Romeo." He smiled at her enough to be polite and focused on the back of Sebastian's head in front of him.

"We're gonna have a real good time tonight," she added and smirked at him as they all waited for Sebastian to push on a metal plate in the wall. Another door slid open to reveal stairs toward the surface.

"That's why I'm here." He turned away from the door and met her gaze. "Only to run."

"Uh-huh."

"Everyone up." Sebastian waved a hand for the rest of them to follow, and all seven practically ran up the stairs toward the fresh air and the sea breeze and the darkness waiting for them at the top.

That had been his assumption, but when they reached the top of the stairs, they'd entered another room. *At least they made this place a maze. Anyone who breaks in here has considerable exploring to do.* The room was completely empty except for a low bench built into the wall beside the door. Romeo stared at that door like his life depended on it.

Sebastian jerked on the handle and pushed the door open to let in a rush of cool night air. "And here we are." The man shrugged, met Romeo's gaze in the darkness, and unbuttoned his pants.

With a smirk, he ripped the borrowed shirt over his head, soon followed by his pants. He was about to leave everything there on the floor until he saw the others—all of them completely naked now—drop their clothes onto the single bench. Quickly, he gathered his and went to join them.

The man with the spiked hair nodded at him beside the bench. "Formalities."

"No problem."

" 'Cause we're not a bunch of animals, right?" The

man widened his eyes, which flashed the bright silver before his shift, and Romeo snorted.

"Hey, Romeo," Sebastian called from where he stood naked beside the open door. "I'm sure you already know, but I'm obligated to say it anyway. Keep up."

A round of soft laughter came from the others, and in the next second, the leader shifted into a huge gray wolf before he darted through the door. The others followed to shift and disappear into the night—one, two, three, four. Finally, only Romeo and Alisha were left. He gestured toward the open door, and she shook her head and stepped back to put him between her and the night. "I'm last— to keep an eye on everyone." She pressed her lips together and winked at him.

Shaking his head, he stepped toward the open door and almost howled into the night air right then. *Sorry to disappoint you, Alisha. Not tonight.* His entire body prickled as he summoned the wolf and let it out. The minute he dropped on all four and raced out of whatever building they'd left and his paws pounded swiftly across the dirt path toward the grass, he smelled Alisha shifting behind him. The female wolf was close on his heels in no time, and it felt uncomfortably like she was hunting him tonight.

None of it mattered. Romeo raced across the ground beneath the Grecian stars, his sight clear and bright and his muscles coiled and ready to move with all the energy that poured through him. The wolves ahead of him paused only briefly at the top of the hill at the edge of the cliffs at the Mediterranean. He pushed himself harder and faster to join them, and before he made it, the massive gray wolf who led them all tonight darted down the other side of the hill toward the sprawling grass and away from the human city.

Tonight, for a few hours at least, he was truly free. And he wasn't alone.

TWENTY-TWO

The large black van stopped at the edge of the road in the middle of nowhere. The desert-like terrain stretched out around it in all directions with very little dotting the endless sprawl to serve as a landmark. But the Black Heron members who toted their most infuriating prisoner around knew exactly where they were.

The driver stepped out of the vehicle and slammed the door behind him. With a wave of his hand, the back doors to the van clicked and flew open on their own. The dark witch's partners opened their own doors and stepped out to help the one who'd claimed leadership over them, only because the other two knew they couldn't beat him in a fight.

Standing in front of the open back doors now, the witch who liked to call himself Charon—although everyone knew that couldn't have been his real name—scowled at the form huddled on the floor in the back of the van. Although they'd covered Greta Antony's head with a thick black fabric bag, he still saw her infuriating grin whenever he looked at her. Even when he slept, sometimes, which was hard enough to do when they were constantly on the move and unable to pull from this witch what they'd taken so easily from all the others. Charon summoned an electric green jolt at the tip of his fingers and flicked it toward her. "Time to move."

His shocking spell coursed through her for a few seconds and elicited a few choking sounds before it fizzled. The witch grunted and sucked in a deep breath through her teeth. "Thanks for the wakeup call." Her voice was muffled through the bag over her head but the biting, unwavering defiance wasn't.

"Shut up." He raised a hand, balled it into a fist, and twisted hard. His spell dragged her across the rough carpet of the vehicle, and with her hands bound in front of her, she wasn't able to keep herself from falling backward. Her head bumped over the edge before she fell out and thumped onto the dirt road.

His two henchmen stared at him in distaste. "Well, what are you waiting for?" He glanced at the witch in the dust with his nostrils flared. "Get her up. It's time to move."

Wordlessly, his underlings stooped to grasp her under her arms and hoist her to her feet. She chuckled derisively beneath the black cloth. "Don't get me wrong," she said as they pushed and pulled her off the road after Charon. "I know it's been a long time for me. But when was the last time either of you boys took a shower?"

Mickey glanced over her head and met Aldorus' gaze.

When his partner simply rolled his eyes, he squeezed Greta's upper arm tighter than he had to and smacked the back of her head with the other hand. "That's enough."

She stumbled forward. "Hey, sorry. It's a little stuffy in here. And I definitely know when I smell my own stinking body." Her bagged head turned toward one of them, then the other. "Who had garlic for lunch?"

Aldorus shook his head, but Mickey lost his patience. He caught the woman by the backs of both arms and shoved her forward. She tripped over her own feet and landed hard on her front, sprawled on the barren land around them. The wind rushed from her lungs, and she willed herself to catch her breath if even only a little. She needed it right now.

Charon whirled to face his inferiors. "What the hell are you doing?"

Mickey jerked a hand at the hooded woman on the ground. "I've spent months listening to this bitch go on and on about absolutely nothing. We should've cut her tongue out when we realized she wasn't gonna stop."

On the ground, Greta let the string of saliva drip from her full mouth and onto the bag over her face, which she'd pressed into the dirt. If these idiots could continue to bicker with each other, she'd have the time she needed to get enough of herself through that black bag and into the dirt.

"Do you think you have it in you to pull the magic out of this woman?" The leader stared at the man who'd lost his cool at the eleventh hour. "We had to bring her all the way out here 'cause no one else can get what we need out of her. Did you suddenly find the solution or what?"

"No." Mickey shook his head and stared at his boss. On the other side of Greta, Aldorus stared into the black distance that stretched ahead of them, his hands clasped behind his back, and ignored everything. "But she's getting to me."

"That's because you have no goddamn clue what you're doing, Mickey. The more she talks, the clearer that is. Quit screwing around and get this bitch where she needs to be. That's it. If you can't pull it together, I'll pull you apart. Got it?"

"Yeah."

"Yeah what?"

"Yeah, I got it, Charon."

"Get her up."

Now satisfied that she'd spit as much as she could into the dirt, Greta whispered the spell she'd been waiting to cast for the last fifteen hours. The end was close, she could feel it, and this was her last chance to do everything she possibly could for Lily. The words passed her lips quickly, trickled through the wet circle on the bag over her face and into the wet soil below it, and seeped into the water from her own body that she'd left there in the earth. When the time was right, Lily would find this last gift, she knew. A tiny glow of light rose below the cloth over her eyes, and she grinned. *Thank the ancestors for quick spellwork.*

Rough hands grasped her arms again and lifted her from where she'd slumped on her chest on the unforgiving soil. "Are you gonna shut up now?"

Greta grinned where they couldn't see it—she would've grinned even without the bag to cover her face—and shrugged. "Are you gonna take a shower?"

Mickey growled and pushed her forward. Aldorus kept a tight enough grip on her other arm that his idiotic associate couldn't push her into the dirt again.

Charon stormed ahead of them, shaking his head. He didn't expect any kind of warm welcome where they were headed, although for months, he'd been the only man dealing with this nightmare of a witch. No, there wouldn't be a celebration for him, but at least in this place, they could do much more with what they had. And as soon as the others found Greta Antony's daughter, they'd all get what they were owed. That was the only reason he tolerated this massive pain in his ass.

The three Black Heron Society members and their captive Optatus witch moved slowly across the barren land, held up by Greta's physical weakness only. The rest of her could endure almost anything—and had.

In the dark of night and the middle of nowhere, Charon raised his hand and muttered the key spell to gain access to their final destination. A dark, orange-brown shimmer flashed in the air directly ahead of him. With a backward glance at his underlings and their prisoner, he rolled his eyes and stepped through the glow. In the next few seconds, all four of them had disappeared through the warded illusion hiding everything else on the other side. Then, there was nothing but the arid, chilled silence of the barren landscape.

LILY LURCHED up from her bed of cushions with a gasp. "Mom." She thought she'd whispered it, but even that echoed in the empty bunker. "Oh, my God." She fought to catch her breath and glanced around her in the light of the magic orbs below the ceiling, which had graciously dimmed themselves to allow for better sleeping. It had worked earlier, but she wouldn't sleep at all now.

"That was real. It was so real. That's...happening right now." The dream about her mom and her captors, about her muttering a spell into saliva and dirt, about the warded illusion spell through which the Black Heron had taken Greta Antony—she knew without a shadow of a doubt that all of it had happened. Was still happening, maybe. "Where are they?"

She crossed her legs beneath her and tried to sift through the memories of that dream. There hadn't been street signs or landmarks or anything recognizable—merely open, barren land and a dirt road with a black van in the middle of nowhere.

A little desperate, she gritted her teeth and tried to remember anything else, but there was nothing. "How am I supposed to find her with that?" She tried to calm her breathing and instead of panicking about what she'd seen, focused on the fact that there was nothing she could do right now. Maybe she could use the heron coin again when she and Romeo returned to the Winnie.

The moment that thought entered her mind, she wished she had the coin with her. She would have given anything to have it. "We're running out of time. I have to know where she is. I have to get there. This—" With a grunt of frustration, she clapped without even thinking. The black cloud spread between her palms to churn and rumble and fill the bunker with the awful noise of it. All she wanted was that damn coin, and the only thing she knew was that this spell made her feel like she was actually accomplishing something. *If I don't have the coin, I can send my own shadow-bird after her. She'll see the raven and will know I'm coming.*

Her arms shook as she pulled her hands farther and farther apart. She felt the shadow-bird stir in her chest, wanting to get free, ready to fly wherever it was toward her mom to let Greta know that her daughter was—

Something shiny and round fell from the spell growing between Lily's hands and thumped onto the cushions below her crossed legs. Startled, she looked down and saw only the dark shape on the pillow. It was far easier to pull back the spell when she wasn't thinking about it. All she had to do was draw away as she stared at whatever her spell had produced. The black cloud coughed out with a puff of black smoke, and that was it.

Lily summoned a small orb of light in her palm and aimed it at the cushions below her crossed legs. The heron coin glinted at her under the magical light, and in an irrational moment of panic, she snuffed the light out too. She couldn't help it. Her automatic reaction was to glance around the empty bunker and hope no one had seen what she'd seen.

"There's no one here, Lily," she muttered into the

semi-darkness. "But it doesn't make me feel any better about what just happened." She summoned the light orb again and stared at the coin lying so innocently on the cushions beneath her. "Not innocent at all. Neither am I, I guess, because I literally summoned you from the Winnie, didn't I?"

Of course, she could have imagined it and her hand wasn't exactly the steadiest as she held her magical light over it. But it almost looked like the heron coin winked at her in the low light of the bunker. "Nope. I can't use this here. I can't..." Lily sighed and clenched her eyes shut. "Mom. What do I do?"

THE SEVEN WOLVES loped up and over the hilltop toward the open door of the single squat building cut into the sloping mountainside. They moved as quickly as they had on their way out, but it was a satisfied run, no longer bursting with pent-up energy and the need to be released.

Romeo panted behind the others as they slowed in front of the building, his body satisfyingly weary from the hours of keeping up with these wolves. Sebastian shifted first, as was his right in this small pack. The man didn't look at any of them as he stepped inside and steadied himself for a moment against the doorframe. The others followed his example quickly and shed fur and paws and sharp teeth one after the other in exchange for skin and two legs. With more than a little reluctance, Romeo let his wolf slip away from him and fought not to lose his balance when he found himself standing feet taller in front of the open doorway. He stepped inside and turned toward the bench against the wall.

"When was the last time you did this?" Sebastian asked, still breathing a little heavily as he dragged his pants on.

He retrieved the pile of his borrowed clothes and stepped into the loose gray trousers first. "Longer than I can remember."

"Man. That's rough."

"Only sometimes." He smirked and pulled the shirt over his head.

"Well, you definitely held your own tonight." The other man clapped him on the back and nodded. "It was good to have you with us."

"Yeah. Thanks."

Alisha stepped up beside him, smirked at him, and made no effort to take her own clothes from the bench. He didn't find it difficult to not look anywhere but at her eyes. Not when all he could think about now was getting back to Lily to wrap an arm around her before he slipped off into exhausted sleep.

"This doesn't have to be the end of the night, you know." She raised a teasing shoulder and grinned.

"I think it does." He offered her a small smile, which was about as much as he could manage after spending all his energy as a wolf. "Thanks for letting me join you guys." He turned and moved toward the others, who'd all gathered at the top of the stairs and waited for her to put her clothes on and join them.

She chuckled softly and slipped into her ridiculously tight jeans before she yanked her shirt over her head. Even now, she wouldn't take her eyes off him when she came to join the rest of her small pack.

"Okay, back to our cave." Sebastian whooped and headed down the staircase. The other werewolves followed although they were far slower going down than they were on the way up.

"Oh, hey." Romeo shook his head at his own forgetfulness. "There was something I wanted to tell you guys. It might help with the whole being underground with a group of witches thing."

The other woman in the pack chuckled behind him. "Did you find some kind of witch-canceling air-freshener?" A ripple of laughter rose at that.

"It doesn't really do anything about the smell. Only about the...effects, I guess."

Sebastian glanced briefly over his shoulder and raised his eyebrows. "So you think you've solved the wolves and magic issue?"

"Well, I spent the last twenty-four hours at least in one of the rooms down here with witches everywhere and felt like a million bucks. So there's that."

The man frowned and turned at the bottom of the staircase to wait until everyone else joined him. "Yeah, let's hear it."

"You're not gonna believe me." He rubbed the back of his neck and smirked. "But I swear, it's almost a cure."

IN THE SHADOWS beyond the single building into which the small werewolf pack had disappeared, a witch of the Black Heron Society stood behind the trees growing from the mountainside. Jeanette had cloaked herself in an illusion and waited for the last three hours after the shifting wolves had first left. But she'd known they'd be back. And, of course, they were.

"What are you hiding?" she muttered as she leaned forward, one hand wrapped around the narrow tree trunk to hold her steady on the hill.

The presence she'd felt there was fading. That stupid little witch had tapped into their mainframe, and she was only one of the Black Heron's few dozen members who'd been close enough to feel the pull of that call. She'd followed the witch's trail all the way to Otiylo, which had taken her two days and a considerable number of headaches. "The best rewards are always worth the biggest headaches, though, aren't they?" Rewards were exactly what she meant to acquire. She'd snatch that little witch everyone thought was so important and deliver the girl herself to the High Seat. That was sure to get her a front-row ticket at the final Harvest, if not first choice of the type of magic she'd coveted for a very long time.

Only the minute she'd arrived in Otiylo, the thick, screaming energy that followed the young witch who'd used one of the Black Heron's artifacts had faded almost completely. Now, it was nothing but a whisper. Jeanette still felt it, though, and she'd find the girl before the trail went cold.

What she couldn't understand was how these idiotic

werewolves were connected to the girl. The trail was strongest right there, and yet there was nothing to show for it but seven dogs returning to their naked forms before disappearing inside. "Someone's hiding her."

A dark shape appeared from thin air beside her, and she turned her head slowly. "Brutus," she said flatly.

"Jeanette."

"I told you not to follow me."

The black-haired werewolf beside her gave her a sickening grin. "I didn't. I followed the girl."

"There's no way you picked up the trail on your own. It's almost cold."

"I can do a few things you can't, witch."

Jeanette rolled her eyes. "Can you do anything with that building?" The werewolves had left the door wide open, and as far as she could tell, they were either irredeemably clueless or really thought they were protected there.

"I can tell you that one of those wolves has a lot of witch on him."

She hissed and turned to glare at him. "What?"

"What do you think an entire pack like that is hiding in there?"

"If the witch we're looking for is down there, why would I let you come with me?"

"Well, for starters, we both know you can't stop me."

With a hiss, she leapt toward him and brought her face mere inches away from his. "And we both know I can make things even worse for you than they already are. Don't push me."

"Relax. We're all in this for the same thing, aren't we? You want the little witch. I want the little witch. The High Seat wants her. I would think you of all people have learned how to play nice to get what you want—for a little while."

The dark witch scoffed and back away. "Not with you."

Brutus chuckled. "So are you waiting for an invitation or what?"

"Something like that." She glanced at the single square building and the open door and knew that the last traces of the connection she'd felt with the relic that little witch had accessed had led her there for a very specific reason.

TWENTY-THREE

L ily knew that as soon as her fingers touched the heron coin, she'd be drawn out of herself and into the network. She hadn't expected it to be so easy or to come to her so naturally as if she'd used it her entire life and simply had to think about what she wanted to make it happen.

She also hadn't expected to be met immediately with the faces of the Black Heron members the second she entered. The darkness didn't meet her first, followed by the blue lights. As soon as she touched the coin, her breath pulled from her lungs and at the same second, two blue-tinted faces stared at her, so very close.

If she'd been in her body, she would have reeled away. A woman with dark, glistening eyes and a cruel smile peered at her from behind two narrow tree trunks. Beside her stood a man with long black hair pulled into a loose ponytail. They both grinned at her.

"Jeanette," the man said, "I think I'll follow you more often from now on."

The woman's grin faded into a scowl of disgust, and she glanced at him. "I told you no. But at least now we know where she is. We're coming for you, little witch."

Her heart pounded in her chest. Whoever these people were, she'd deal with them later. Right now, she had to find her mom. After her dream, she knew there was very little time for her to do anything else. Finding Greta was all that mattered.

As soon as she had the thought, the blue-glowing faces vanished and she was sucked through the tunnel-like expanse like before. This time, the vision following her mom took her farther south, out of Greece and across the Mediterranean and into Libya. She knew she had to focus on what exactly she saw, which was more or less like a map of Europe but without any direct routes or labeled high-ways. The network's traveling tunnel panned out to show her something like a desert, then zoomed in as far as it would go.

Entirely focused on her search, she stared at the same dirt road of her dream, only this one didn't have a van pulled off into the dirt. There the same expanse of nothingness, the same lack of landmarks, and nothing else to tell her where to go but a faded, orange-brown shimmer in the air. Something on the ground in front of her started to glow.

She wanted to reach out and touch the light in the dirt. *If I can touch that, I'll know where she is.* Her fingers stretched toward the light and her actual fingers in her physical body pulled away from the coin.

"Crap." She glanced around the dark bunker and sighed in frustration. "That's not what I wanted at all. There's gotta be a better way to find out what I need to—"

She stopped abruptly when a tingling itch crawled up the back of her spine until it settled at the base of her skull. "Oh, no." Maybe it was the fact that she'd now used the heron coin three times and had begun to connect with it like the real society members. Maybe being down there for almost two days had heightened her senses. But the instant that prickle of awareness settled in the back of her head, she knew.

"No. No, no, no." She leapt to her feet, wobbled a little on the cushions, and kicked one of them on top of the heron coin. She didn't want to look at it or think about it because now she knew it had definitely been the wrong choice. "Hey!" She scrambled off the cushions, dashed across the large, empty room, and searched for the doors that slid back into tunnels she hadn't yet seen. "Can anyone hear me? Is anyone there? Hey!" Her fists pounded on the thick stone walls that scraped at her skin, but that was obviously the least effective way to get anyone's attention.

With a deep breath, she summoned the revealing spell with the soft yellow glow that flared in her palm. "If this is good enough to find a secret message hidden inside a wall in Colorado, it's good enough to find a hidden door." She ran her hand over the wall, which under the low light of the orbs that floated above her looked as seamless as if she'd been sealed inside a very large coffin. "Stop thinking like that, Lily. You still have time."

The minute the yellow glow of her spell caught the seal of the first door she found, the entire outline of the door illuminated with purple light. "Okay." Before she could think how to open it—which seemed to answer only to the witches who'd been down there way longer than she had—it pushed back from the wall and slid open all on its own. "Hey. Hey, who's in there?"

"Lily?" Romeo's face came into view as it opened fully. "Hey, what's wrong?"

"I messed up. I—" She saw the other werewolf standing behind him, who made the same face as her friend did. Pointing at him, she asked, "Do you know how to get to Ozias? And everyone else in here?"

"Yeah."

"Go wake them up. Go tell them—"

"Hold on, Lil. Will you tell me what's happening first?"

"No. Tell them the Black Heron's close and they found out how to get in and they're coming. Right now!"

The other werewolf startled a little in surprise, then nodded and turned down the dark passage to disappear into the darkness.

Lily whirled away from the tunnel and paced across the bunker, clutching her forehead.

"Are you serious?" Romeo came up behind her and tried to get her to look at him. "How do you know they're coming?"

"I..." She clenched her eyes shut and took a deep

breath. "I had a dream. About my mom—where they took her. And then I used the coin to make sure. The network showed me the identical thing. I think she's in the most dangerous place for her, and I couldn't wait any longer to find out where that is because we have to get there, Romeo. We have to get her out."

"Woah, woah. Hold on." He caught her upper arms, stopped her in her tracks, and turned her toward him. "Lily, you left the coin in the Winnie."

"I know. And I was trying to summon my shadow-bird. I thought maybe that would help her. Or at least let her know that I know and also let her know that we haven't given up." She gritted her teeth against the pounding headache that built steadily behind her eyes. "The black cloud. It didn't summon the raven, Romeo. It brought me the heron coin."

"What?"

"It dropped it right in my lap, and I...I don't know. I honestly don't know how. But I couldn't simply sit there."

"You used it."

"I'm so sorry."

He ran a hand over his mouth and sighed. "Okay. Come here." He led her quickly across the bunker toward the other wall and pointed. "There's another door here, I think. I saw someone use it earlier. Find it and put up whatever kind of ward you can. If the Black Heron's coming right now, we can at least try to be ready for them."

"Yeah. Yeah, you're right." *And here he is to pull me out of it again.* Lily nodded and only had to search the wall for a few seconds before she found the other door. Quickly, she tapped each corner of it, where a bright red light illuminated and remained lit. Then, she drew the most powerful warding symbols she knew on the surface, which pulled at her touch with the same red light.

"There's another one over here," Romeo said. "I think. Somewhere here." He waved his hand at another section of the same wall and moved on to find the other doors. She located that one quickly enough too and immediately cast the same ward around it.

Pounding footsteps echoed through the passage toward the open doorway, then Ozias burst into the empty bunker and stared with wide eyes at Lily's completed ward. "I just heard."

She turned and swallowed her guilt. "I'll have these up everywhere I can."

"Good." The bearded man raised his hand and pointed multiple times around the huge room. With each flick of his finger, another door illuminated. There were nine in total, including the ones she had already warded. "They don't all lead aboveground, but it's better to shut off as much of this place as we can. Sebastian and Cosima are waking the others."

"No." Lily finished the second warded door and turned to approach Ozias. "Don't bring anyone else in here. This is my fault, and I don't want any of you to suffer for my...really horrible choice. I'm so sorry—"

"Stop." The man set a gentle hand on her shoulder, held her gaze, and nodded. "We knew the dangers when we offered you a place to stay. I know that whatever you did, Lily, you didn't do it with the intention to hurt us here.

And even as an Optatus, you can't stand against the Black Heron on your own. I doubt all of them will be here, but any number of them is enough. We'll stand with you. If those people succeed in their goals, they'll break our pact anyway. I'd rather fight them for a good reason than merely because I trusted too much in blood magic."

She licked her lips and nodded. "Okay. Is there a door that's... I don't know. Most visible? Somewhere they'd be most likely to enter? They know I'm here. I simply want to make sure they come for me rather than anyone else down here."

"I don't know." The old man's eyes widened, and he shook his head. "We have at least five passages to the surface, and—"

"The stairs." Romeo turned away from the walls and jogged toward them. "Sebastian led us up a set of stairs to this...building. That's where we—" He cleared his throat. "I don't think anyone shut the door."

"Did anyone see you?" Ozias' brows drew together in concern.

"I...I have no idea." He glanced from the old man to Lily. "I was so exhausted, I—"

A scream sounded from the other end of the dark passage and echoed toward the central area which, empty as it now was of all the usual bustle, seemed to capture and amplify the sound.

All three of them shared a glance before the old man raced down the passage. "Ward the four corners," he shouted over his shoulder. "We'll face them where you are." He vanished into the darkness, and a massive explosion followed by cracking and crumbling stone filled the air.

"We have to go with him." Lily moved forward, but Romeo caught her arm.

"Lily, there are more magicals behind these doors in here than there are down that one tunnel. The werewolves down there can take care of themselves long enough to get back here and fight with us. Everyone else... They need you to put wards on those doors and keep them safe. We'll make sure none of those society bastards get past us, I promise. But you need to do the doors first."

"Right." With a brisk nod, she turned and rushed toward the next door, choosing to ward the corners first as Ozias had instructed. *This is better. This I can do. It's a plan.* It wasn't as easy to work the way she wanted while the sounds of a battle echoed to her from the other end of that long, dark tunnel. Werewolves snarled and growled, spells crashed into walls and doorways, and feet pounded down stairs and along the tunnel toward them. It sounded like a thousand voices shouted from the other side of that narrow space, and she forced herself to focus on the one thing she knew she could do right now. *If I can make complicated wards with that as background noise, I can do anything.*

She was almost finished with the third corner door by the time the resident magicals flooded into the main central bunker. Most of them looked terrified, some of them merely angry, and a few were covered in a fine white dust the color of the walls. But as soon as they spilled into the main room, they regrouped, readied themselves, and turned to face the dark tunnel. They'd make another stand there.

"How many more are out there?" Romeo asked one of the closest witches.

The woman closed her eyes briefly and counted in her head. "Maybe a dozen. The werewolves are holding most of them back for now. Ozias is—"

Another loud explosion sounded, followed by a bitter scream of rage, and muffled voices rose behind it. Cosima darted out of the tunnel, followed by a puff of more fine white dust that settled into her pitch-black braid. She coughed a few times, glanced around, and settled on her gaze on Lily. "Are you almost done?"

She finished the third door and stepped away. "Only one more."

"Good. Don't stop." The woman raised her fist, shook it, and the blazing purple trident her family had summoned for centuries materialized in her hand again. "I prefer to use this outside and near the ocean if I can." She scowled and her expression settled into hard lines. "But it's not entirely useless underground, either."

Lily darted toward the final corner door and set to work building the last ward.

Three wolves darted through the entrance into the main room, one of them with a slight limp but well enough to keep going on his own. Romeo retreated to the pile of cushions against the far wall and undressed while everyone's attention was on the tunnel. Not that he cared about stripping down in front of a group of strangers but because he wanted to see that damn coin for himself. He stepped out of his borrowed trousers and kicked them to where he knew Lily had been sleeping. His shirt dropped to the floor and he found it buried beneath two gold-embroidered pillows. With a grimace, he stooped to pick up the heron coin and shoved it quickly into the pocket of his pants. When he dropped those again, he finally let himself shift.

More shouts rose in the darkness. Ozias' voice thundered above all of them, clearly recognizable in words and tone. The explosions continued before someone else shouted, "Hurry. Pick her up!"

Sebastian barreled into the main room and immediately shifted into his huge gray wolf. Behind him came another man, completely naked, with a naked woman slung over his shoulder. She was out cold, her brown curly hair bouncing as the other werewolf tried to run and carry her at the same time.

"How is she?" Cosima called.

The werewolf grunted at her. "She hit her head—hard, so she's out."

"Put her over there." The woman nodded at the pile of cushions, and the curly-haired werewolf was placed gently on the pile before her rescuer shifted into a thin wolf with patchy fur of red and brown.

The six wolves gathered in a staggered line between the tensely waiting witches and the tunnel. Romeo crouched and growled at the flashing lights that grew closer through the well of blackness. All around the room, the defenders prepared their own attack spells—churning flames in every color, crackling bolts of magical energy, and shimmering lights that would do as much damage in one form or another. One woman brandished a whip in one hand, which twitched all on its own as it hung at her side, covered in brilliant flashes of purple light.

Ozias' voice roared with incomprehensible words through the tunnel, and a flash of purple and silver illuminated the entire passage. At least half a dozen dark-spirited magicals stood on the other side of him and hurled their attack spells at the man who'd dedicated his life to his town and his country and any magical within them he could protect. His own version of the purple trident flared to life in his hand, and he pounded the butt of it on the tunnel floor. Purple light strobed toward his enemies and held them back long enough for the man to turn and race down the remaining stretch toward his waiting people.

The Black Heron members shouted and raged on the other side of the man's temporary shield and Ozias burst into the main room with his purple trident in hand. Cosima snapped her fingers, and the door into the central bunker slid along the wall to return to its place with a resounding boom.

The noises in the tunnel were definitely muted after that, but everyone waiting there knew it wouldn't be long before the magicals who had targeted Lily Antony made their way past all the last-minute defenses. Ozias squared his feet and faced the closed door, held his trident aloft, and closed his eyes. The spell he muttered wasn't for anyone else's ears, but his daughter took her place beside him and joined in. The only thing anyone else could do was wait.

As soon as Lily finished the last ward on the fourth

corner door, she took a last glance at the glowing red runes and nodded. Satisfied, she joined the other witches and summoned her favorite sparking-red attack spell in both palms. A few of the witches caught her eye and nodded in stern determination. She nodded in return. *None of them have any idea that I did this. At least I can fight with them.* She stepped around the gathered witches and stopped on the other side of Romeo, putting herself in what was now the front line of this fight. He turned his huge black head to gaze at her with silver eyes and licked his muzzle.

"Yeah." She nodded. "We got this." Taking a deep breath, she watched the door to the tunnel, which had now taken on a shimmering purple glow from Ozias' and Cosima's spell. After a second, both father and daughter retracted their outstretched tridents and opened their eyes. They stepped back on the other side of the line of werewolves and waited with everyone else.

"We all wanted to take a stand, didn't we?" he shouted without turning around. A few shouts of agreement rose from the witches gathered behind him, although they only numbered a few dozen. From the sounds that drifted toward them from the other side of the door, even as muffled as they were, it sounded like they faced at least that many Black Heron magicals, if not more. The bearded man nodded and grasped his trident with both hands. "Now's as good a time as any."

TWENTY-FOUR

The voices, pounding footsteps, and launched spells grew louder with every second on the other side of the barrier. Whatever their attackers launched struck the closed door with a sizzling crack. It shuddered and the purple glow created by Ozias and Cosima flickered under the pressure before it flared defiantly to life again.

Lily flexed her fingers and the red sparks crackled along their tips. The waiting was the worst part. Twice more, a massive spell was hurled at the other side of the door. The room around them seemed to shudder this time and released small waves of the same fine white dust to drift around them.

"It won't hold forever, will it?" an older man asked.

"Definitely not," Ozias replied and pressed his lips together. "This is as prepared as we can—"

The door broke under the strain and it seemed like a part of the wall exploded in a burst of sparks and green flame. Huge chunks careened through the room. The wolves scattered, and Lily dropped her attack spell in order to join Ozias and Cosima to catch as much of the debris as they could before it injured any of the witches unlucky enough to be caught in its path. She pulled two stone projectiles from the air and gestured with her hands toward the far wall beside her. The witches stepped out of the way, but none of them lost their nerve.

The dark opening of the tunnel smoked and crackled with green and purple light like a handful of electrical wires had been ripped free and left to dangle in mid-air, sparking dangerously. This was merely the end of a Black Heron witch's spell that had battled Ozias' door protection within the smoking haze. The purple sparks died out, the green flared to life even stronger now, and a darkened form stepped through the blackness.

They'd all had time to prepare as much as they could for the battle everyone knew was inevitable, but that didn't make the first foray from their enemy any less surprising. A blast of green light hurtled through the doorway and flung several witches off their feet and across the room. Flames immediately followed, and there was a moment of consternation before the defenders found their bearings.

Lily launched both her attack spells into the entrance but was unable to see whether they actually found a target. Her response was much the same as everyone was doing—throwing spells in the hope that they would have a real effect. Shouts responded from the tunnel and more of the walls on either side of the damaged door burst inward. The room filled with fine dust and smoke, illuminated by blazing streaks of spells in every color exchanged between the two ranks of witches. The first wave of Black Heron members stepped through the doorway they'd widened for themselves with determined scowls and immediately delivered a barrage of spells.

The wolves had the opportunity to attack and they leapt at the closest enemies and managed to fell a few of the invaders. They served as enough of a distraction. The dark magicals directed their efforts to fight the huge beasts instead, which enabled Ozias and his witches to throw everything they had at the intruders. Lily fired every powerful spell she could think of at the approaching line of wizards and a few warlocks. Thanks to her earlier encounter with the Black Heron members a few nights before, the presence of these red-eyed beings wasn't unexpected.

Even the four werewolves who darted out of the tunnel to attack those fighting with Romeo made sense. Of course, the Black Heron had werewolves in their ranks too. But no one could have anticipated the massive hulk of black fur that emerged from the expanded tunnel moments later.

"What the hell is that?" a witch shouted beside Lily.

"I don't—hey!" She raised a warded shielded hastily before the witch who'd spoken would have caught an inky, tar-like sludge in the face. The goo slid off the shield and splattered on the floor, where it immediately ate through the stone and would probably continue to burn a hole for a fair distance. The woman nodded her thanks and turned to throw a few attacks of what looked like glass shards.

She tried to keep an eye on the other witches and to protect them with her warded shields where she could. It didn't seem like many others knew that kind of defensive spell but she was good at casting those. Her gaze flicked constantly toward the hulking, hairy beast that lumbered into the room and swatted at anyone and everyone within its reach.

That's like a werewolf on steroids. She summoned a whirl of blue flames on the jacket of a warlock who'd settled his red-eyed gaze on her. He shouted in surprise and batted at his clothes before someone else's spell hurtled him against the nearby wall.

The massive black abomination uttered a roar that stopped almost everyone in their tracks, including the Black Heron magicals fighting with it.

The immobilizing shock only lasted a few seconds before one of the werewolves leapt toward the beast and latched onto it with intensely strong jaws. The creature roared again and swatted the wolf aside with a paw that seemed to be the size of the wolf that had attempted the attack.

"Destroy that thing!" Ozias bellowed. The tips of his trident launched a volley of purple streams like a machine gun. The onslaught struck the monster in the side and it staggered against the far wall, only feet from the pile of cushions and the injured werewolf who'd been laid there in supposed safety. The wall shuddered beneath the beast's weight, but it regained its feet. It seemed even angrier now and turned its blazing red eyes onto the central group of defending witches.

"We don't have enough," Lily muttered as the colossus swiped claws at the wolves attacking it. Romeo and the others were fast enough to escape most of the blows, and those who were batted aside were strong enough to take a strike and regroup. That wouldn't last forever, though.

Now, the defending witches were divided between attacking the massive werewolf who never should have been that size and the few dozen Black Heron magicals who continued an unremitting fusillade of attacks at them. Lily faced a snarling witch with scars crisscrossing half his face and neck. The man sneered at her and widened his eyes. "Thanks for the invitation."

She delivered a blast of electric-green curses at his face. Only the first one hit home but glancing off his ear before he deflected the others with his own shield. The scars on that side of his face glowed green for a few seconds, then died away.

"You're still so clueless, aren't you?" He raised his hand and spread his fingers. Tendrils of blackish-green snaked from beneath his fingernails and lashed out at her face, arms, and legs. She blasted them away as best she could and discovered after two attempts that the blue fire worked best. He shouted in rage and ejected the same vine-like tendrils from his other hand. She folded her arms and summoned the strongest of her warded shields, which sparked and knocked her back every time another of the strange appendages struck with a sharp tap like metal on glass.

She staggered back under his constant attack and protected herself long enough for the gray wolf who led the pack in Otiylo to launch himself at her attacker. Sebastian and the leering witch tumbled onto the floor together. The wolf snarled and the scarred man flung bursts of spells he couldn't quite aim the way he needed to. Lily called her red sparks up again and brought them together, planning to blast them into the witch while he was on the floor.

Something sliced into her shoulder, and she cried out, her spell forgotten. She smelled burning flesh and thought she'd felt the worst of it until whatever spell had found purchase began to really eat away at her nerves. A burning agony unlike anything she could have imagined flared.

Her teeth gritted, she glared at the witch with the dark hair—the same one she'd seen first in the Black Heron network less than an hour before. Jeanette stepped slowly toward her, completely ignoring the powerful magic flung in all directions and which steadily damaged parts of the bunker now too. A huge sheet of the ceiling crashed behind her as she stalked toward Lily, and the woman didn't even bat an eyelid.

"That'll slow you down." The witch's lips pulled into the same cruel smile she had seen in the network. "Although you've done enough of that yourself, haven't you?"

The massive, obviously enhanced werewolf impacted with another wall and prompted warning shouts as the defending witches tried to take advantage of its momentary weakness.

"You simply couldn't stay away." The Black Heron witch flicked her wrist and a wickedly jagged, jet-black dagger appeared in her hand. The tip of the blade dripped liquid fire, and each of the drops inched their way toward her quarry.

Lily tried to raise her arms to cast whatever defensive spell she could, but the agony in her wounded shoulder made it almost impossible to move at all. She could only reverse slowly away from her imposing adversary and the burning trails of liquid fire that slithered across the floor.

"That's good," the woman continued smugly. That'll make it so much easier for you to give in completely when we pull the magic out of you. Torren assumed your failure of a mother had the last thing we needed. I think it's you." The witch tossed her black knife and caught it again in an underhand grip. "I might cut you a little first for fun, though."

Lily's back pressed against the wall, and she had nowhere else to go.

Voices rose again from the other side of the bunker. The shouts turned to screams quickly, and she turned her head as much as she could.

Three warlocks stood together, chanting with their arms raised from their sides. A red, swirling mist drifted from their open palms in whirls of blood magic, which had already reached the defending witches and a few of Sebastian's werewolves. The red mists snaked across throats and around arms and dug into fur and flesh alike. The wolves squealed in agony, which was enough to prove that whatever the awful warlock spell was, it was bad.

Jeanette stopped to watch the torture. She threw her head back and cackled when Sebastian crumpled. All four of the gray wolf's legs twitched in agony as the blood-mist swarmed over his body. "Look at that." She pointed and doubled over in laughter. "They have you to thank for that.

There's nothing down here to stop what those warlocks unleashed. They're disgusting, yeah." She scowled at her three allies and shrugged. "But they do get the job done. You will too when we've used you up." With a grin, she inclined her head and stalked toward Lily again.

The young witch steeled herself and gave up any attempt to use the spells she'd practiced for half her life. They simply weren't enough. She tried to bring her hands together for the black cloud, but her left arm wouldn't move at all now beneath the blazing pain in her shoulder. Her tormentor clicked her tongue a second before Romeo's shaggy form hurtled in a blur of black and pounded into the back wall on the other side of the bunker.

All the screams and the agonized cries of the magicals who'd stood with her—despite her awful mistake—stoked a fire of defiant rage inside her. *I won't let it end like this.* She waited until Jeanette was almost upon her, and as the Black Heron witch raised the jagged dagger for a striking blow, she dropped to the ground. Her dive landed her on her wounded shoulder, which brought a blood-curdling scream from her throat. Somehow, she managed to move beyond it and kicked the dark witch's legs as hard as she could. She hadn't exactly aimed at the kneecap, but she heard it snap all the same. The witch screamed and fell back. Despite the almost unbearable pain, Lily managed to bring her right hand down upon her left where it lay against the debris-strewn floor.

The pain erupted in her shoulder tenfold, but she raised her good hand slowly while she lay on her side and brought her black cloud into existence one again. The darkness churned and roared between her palms, and her determined scream only added fuel to the growling black storm that roiled and writhed between her hands. Her entire body flared with excruciating pain and she could barely feel her shoulder, but she somehow managed to raise her good arm all the way up before she released the shadowed power on the only magicals who really deserved it.

The darkness ballooned toward the bunker's ceiling and spread like a stain in all directions until it blocked everything from her view. The bunker fell silent for a moment with surprise as the fighting magicals not already close to defeat paused to look at the power that built before their eyes. The dark spell flashed with dangerous streaks of light, some bright white and others with a dark absence of light altogether.

A cold hand dug painful fingers into Lily's ankle. She glanced down and saw Jeanette, the witch's jaw set in pain and determination, trying to claw her way up the leg to reach her. She lowered her hand toward the Black Heron member and drew a churning streak of her dark spell away from the main body. It caught the other woman in the hollow of her throat, and her adversary uttered another scream before the still expanding spell hid her from sight as well. She thought she heard her adversary choke, the scream muffled by the power of the spell, but she didn't care. With her good hand, she commanded her most powerful spell to do its worst to the Black Heron.

The massive, grotesque werewolf snarled and snapped at the spell-storm, but he found no purchase in a cloud of unbelievable power. A trembling howl escaped his throat, and he thrashed against the walls where he'd been cornered before he fell and writhed on the floor. The bunker shuddered again and the screams grew louder, but they weren't from her allies this time.

Muted colors of witch and warlock spells flared against the billowing darkness that filled almost half the room in front of her. The first defender to make it through was Romeo. He leapt through it, shook himself wildly, and padded toward Lily on swift paws. Three other wolves followed, joined soon after by Ozias and Cosima and the others who'd fought beside them. Most of the residents staggered through the blackness and assisted one another where necessary before they stopped and turned to stare at what she had unleashed.

"Be careful," she shouted and tried to push herself up to lean against the wall. "It's not over."

The first of the warlocks stumbled through the ebony shroud and fell on his knees. His glowing red eyes settled on her, and he snarled before he completely vanished. What remained of the Black Heron's attack to kidnap her thrust through the spell in twos and threes. A few of them launched last-effort attacks at the defenders grouped as a silent audience, but Ozias' people hadn't been attacked the way their enemy had. A few witches beside Lily only had to fire a few spells before, one by one, the enemy magicals teleported out of the bunker to avoid the inevitable destruction they faced if they remained. None of them looked happy about leaving without their prize but it was better than not leaving at all.

In that moment, part of Lily wished they didn't still have the choice. *No. That's not the way this works. Not for me.* 'Good intentions turned bad,' Galen had said. *Let them crawl back to wherever they came from, then. Now, they know what I can do.*

Barely a few seconds later, all the invaders had taken their leave of the underground safe house they'd been so sure they could overrun. She couldn't be entirely sure, but it certainly seemed that all the defending magicals had absolutely no doubt as to what had been accomplished. Her black cloud now shrank and closed in on itself as if it were a pile of dirt sucked up by a vacuum, When it was nothing more than a tiny speck, a whispering cough sounded and the last traces of shadowed smoke curled into an inward spiral until that was gone too.

It left behind a number of bodies, which wasn't at all surprising in a battle like this. *It's so much like Ichacál and definitely not even close.* In the supposed healing temple in Guatemala, the death witch Neron had done the heavy lifting for all of them in the end. A witch had sacrificed her already fading life so he could use his magic to aid the others. With it, he'd obliterated the Wisemen and freed the magicals who'd been locked in cages beneath the temple for longer than anyone cared to admit.

But in the bunker, everyone had done their part. It was impossible to tell which witch or werewolf had eliminated any particular Black Heron enemy now sprawled in the dust and amongst the rubble in the subterranean chamber. Only Lily could pinpoint exactly who had fallen to her black-cloud spell.

The body of the same man she had seen in the network lay where the monstrous werewolf had breathed his last in the far corner. His long black ponytail was splayed across the floor behind him and matted with who knew how many people's blood.

Breathing heavily, she looked behind her again and her gaze settled on Jeanette. The dark witch's hand had frozen in the same claw that had grasped her ankle, her mouth open in the scream she'd given as she died. The woman's eyes were still open too, but they were lifeless. She closed her eyes and turned her head away.

No one spoke as they gazed at all the damage. Cosima groaned and raced across the bunker. She dropped to her knees in front of a naked body on the ground, and Lily couldn't see past the woman to discover who it was. On the other side of the scattered cushions, Romeo dug through the few pillows strewn about and found his clothes. With wide eyes, he stared at the body in front of the older witch while he tugged his clothes on. The other werewolves did the same, although one of them with short, spiked blond hair didn't bother to dress and instead, slid across the floor on the other side of the body and wailed over the person curled on the floor.

The flaring pain in Lily's shoulder had grown into a vague numbness and her arm hung limply at her side as she pushed herself against the wall and to her feet. *Not him. Please, not him.* She shuffled past the other magicals who stared in shock at the friend they'd lost.

"Lily." Ozias walked slowly toward her. "Let me take a look at your arm."

"Not yet." She tried to move past him, but he settled his hand on her other shoulder and stopped her.

"It looks bad. We need to tend to that."

"I'm fine. I need to see." Her teeth gritted, she jerked her shoulder away from the old man and approached Cosima and the still-naked werewolf kneeling beside the body. Romeo headed toward her with wide eyes and glanced from Sebastian's body to her. "No." She swallowed thickly and couldn't believe what she saw. "No, he...he helped me. He was..." She grimaced and moved closer.

"Lily, there's nothing—"

"No, I can fix this. I can—" Her good hand went to the mirror charm at her throat that let her undo the most powerful spell cast. In the back of her mind, she didn't really think that the warlocks' blood magic—which must have been what killed Sebastian—was the most powerful spell cast in this bunker. *I have to try.* She stopped at his bare feet and clenched the mirror charm in her hand as she closed her eyes. *Unravel the most powerful setback...* A faint silver glow rose from within her closed fist and as quickly, it was gone.

Nothing happened and no one moved, especially not Sebastian.

"That's not right." She took a shuddering breath and felt her knees weaken beneath her. "It should've worked. It's supposed to bring him—" Suddenly, her head was swimming and her knees buckled a second later.

Romeo caught her before she fell and led her toward the scattered cushions near the still-naked werewolf woman who'd been unconscious during the entire battle.

She didn't feel his hand on her shoulder as he guided her and really didn't feel much of anything when she eased back on the cushions.

"Hey," he shouted. "We need help over here."

The bunker seemed to burst into life again with rising voices and quickly moving people. She sighed and slipped into oblivion where her body didn't hurt anymore.

TWENTY-FIVE

L ily woke feeling like she'd been wrapped in too many blankets. When she managed to open her eyes and glance at her body, it turned out she was actually cocooned. "What the—" She tried to wiggle her arms out of the adult-witch swaddle someone had been ridiculous enough to put her in, but she couldn't move. "Um...hello? Can anyone come to untie me, please?"

Someone snorted behind her and the mattress beneath her shifted a little before Romeo poked his head over hers and smiled sleepily at her. "You're up. How do you feel?"

"Like a sushi roll."

With a chuckle, he slid off the bed and smoothed the hair away from her face. "I'm gonna go get Donna and ask if it's okay to unwrap you."

"Is she the person who said this was a good idea?"

He grinned and nodded. "Yep. It probably saved your life, too. I'll let her explain it." He patted the mattress beside her as if telling her to stay where she was—like she had any choice— turned, and headed toward the door to the small room.

"Wait, where are we?"

"Oh. Uh, I think it's Ozias' old house. Or Cosima's. Something like that."

"We're not underground anymore?"

Romeo shook his head. "They were out of extra rooms seeing as our little battle destroyed most of them."

"But the Black Heron's gonna come back, Romeo, because I used the coin. They know where I—"

"Woah, woah. Slow down." He returned to the bed and leaned over her again to hold her gaze. "Lemme go get Donna first, okay? Then we'll explain why it's totally okay for you to be in a real bed wrapped like a sushi roll."

She snorted. "It's really hard to argue with you when I can't move."

"I know. I'll be right back." He slipped through the door and left her alone in a room where real sunlight actually spilled through the windows and a fresh sea breeze teased in through the narrow openings where they stood ajar. "I didn't think I'd be out from underground so soon..." She tried to wiggle around again to free her arms even a little, but the blankets wouldn't budge an inch. "Okay. More waiting."

Five minutes later, the werewolf returned with a spring in his step and a short, round woman with gray streaks in her long, dark hair. "Are you Donna?" Lily asked. "I would really like to get out of these blankets."

The woman chuckled, nodded, and folded her hands over her rather large belly. "It looks like it worked very well."

"Well enough to unwrap me?" Unable to wave her arms around like she would have liked, she had to content herself with moving her head instead.

"Okay, well quit moving around like that until I tell you you're good to go, huh?" Donna approached the bed and peered over her nose at Lily's tightly swaddled body as if she were looking beneath a pair of glasses. She pressed the back of her hand to the girl's forehead, nodded, and poked her finger in the young witch's ear.

"Hey." She jerked her head away and frowned at the woman.

"Just checking." Donna grinned. She cleared her throat, raised both hands over her patient's chest, and muttered an unintelligible incantation. A soft purple light rose from her palms, and a warmth spread over her chest, across her shoulders, and up toward the back of her head. The healing witch's hands moved gently up and down her patient's body before they both focused on her left shoulder and the magical wound the Black Heron witch Jeanette had left there. "What do you feel here?"

"Uh...a little tingle. That's it."

"Good." The woman ended her spell and the light disappeared. She smiled at Lily before she flicked the young witch's injured shoulder with all her fingers at once.

"Ow. Yeah, that still hurts a little."

"Also good." The healer chuckled and nodded. "You'll

be fine. Up you go." She shoved her hand under her back and helped the patient sit in bed before she began to unwind the tightly wrapped blankets. She wasn't particularly gentle about it either and jerked the coverings around and around while Lily simply sat there like a dashboard bobblehead doll. "Okay, move slowly. Do you understand me?" The woman pressed her left arm down at her side and held her gaze until she nodded to the healer's satisfaction.

Once Donna released her arm, Lily glanced at Romeo and gave her arm an experimental flex. Her shoulder was definitely sore but it was nothing compared to the agony of the night before. *Or maybe it's been longer than that.* "How long have I been out?" She poked and prodded at her shoulder, where she'd been sure Jeanette's spell had torn through her skin and probably burned her.

"About fourteen hours," the healer said with a curt nod.

"That's it?"

He chuckled. "You healed almost as fast as a werewolf."

"Yeah. Ten times slower is almost as fast." Her sarcasm sent them both into a round of soft laughter. She turned to smile at the healer. "What was it, exactly, that…knocked me out?"

"That wound on your shoulder."

"I know, but—"

"A curse, a little poison, and considerable dark magic." Donna nodded slowly and studied the injured arm. "It left a scar, though. And that will be there forever, as scars tend to be."

"Oh." She pulled the sleeve of her t-shirt down to see the long, bright pink slash that curved over her left shoulder. "It's a big one."

"Not too big to mend. You should take it easy for another twenty-four hours after this." The woman caught her wrist but kept her other hand on the healed shoulder and raised the young witch's arm to test it for herself. "I'd like to say my healing is instantaneous, but I'd be lying to... well, almost everyone." She gave her an oddly sarcastic smile, dropped her patient's arm, and stepped back. "You can head out any time you like, Lily. But take it easy—"

"For the next twenty-four hours. Yep." Lily tucked her hair behind her ears and nodded. "Thank you, Donna."

"Thank you. You did more than enough to pay for all my good work." The heavyset witch winked, flashed Romeo a grin, then turned and walked out of the bedroom.

"And she does good work, doesn't she?" He approached the bed and pulled the sleeve of her shirt down a little to see her scar for himself. His low whistle and nod seemed to indicate that he was impressed. "That looked nasty when you passed out."

"I promise you, it felt even worse."

He snorted and leaned down to kiss the bright pink flesh on her shoulder. "I bet. What you did, Lil..." He lifted his head, looked her in the eye, and raised his eyebrows. "That was incredible."

"It was...weird." She shrugged and couldn't help but

smile at the admiration reflected in his eyes. "Okay, maybe a little incredible. What about Sebastian? Did he..."

His eyes narrowed for a moment before he looked down and took her hand. "No. There wasn't anything you could do."

She swallowed thickly and squeezed his hand. "I knew that I think. But I still had to try, you know? I had to see if I could undo the warlocks' spell that killed him. He...he tackled a seriously intense witch for me and helped me to stay in the fight a little longer. I wish I could have done the same thing for him."

"I know." Romeo rubbed his mouth as he stared at the comforter, then looked up again and tucked more hair behind her hear. "But you took care of everyone else. Sebastian was the only one who didn't make it, and for the kind of fight that was, I'd say it's better than anyone expected."

"That doesn't mean he deserved to go like that."

"No. No one does." He paused and grimaced. "Except for that monster wolf-thing, maybe."

Lily grunted both distaste and agreement. "Another magical Frankenstein, huh? That was disgusting."

"Yeah, I might have nightmares." He took a deep breath and looked at her again, and she thought he might have been serious. "But everyone else is safe. And you kicked serious Black Heron ass down there, Lil."

"Please don't give me all the credit for that. It wasn't only me. And we wouldn't have even had to fight if I hadn't chosen to use that stupid coin like an idiot."

"Which none of my people are aware of, by the way."

Ozias stepped through the open doorway into the bedroom. He limped a little but otherwise looked fine. "I plan to keep it that way."

She stared at the bearded man and tried to smile. "Why?"

"Because, Lily, you are something incredibly special." He stopped at her bedside and studied her face with a gentle smile. "I've heard the stories of Optatus witches—the adventurous tales and the lessons of warning and caution. None of them said a thing about Optatus magic being as...discerning as your spell was last night. I was afraid of it when you showed me on your first night here. Now, honestly, I'd feel much better if you stuck around." She opened her mouth to protest but he raised a finger and added, "But I know you still have a long road ahead of you. Definitely within yourself if not in physical distance, depending on where you're headed next. Did you find your mother?"

Pressing her lips together, Lily nodded. "I saw her, yeah. And where she is now. At least, where she was when I used the coin."

"Is it any place I might know?"

She chuckled wryly. "That depends on how well you know nondescript dirt roads in the middle of nowhere in Libya."

"Ah. There might be too many of those for me to narrow down for you, Lily. I'm sorry."

"Don't be. I'm simply gonna have to find a different way to look for her. If she's still where I saw them take her,

I don't know if the coin's gonna be able to help me much more. Maybe. We'll see."

"I have no doubt you'll find your way. You have so much riding on this, my dear. And you have considerable power too. That doesn't always make for the most stable combination, but I have every confidence that you'll pull through."

"Thank you." She frowned and glanced at Romeo. "I, uh...I do have one more question, though."

"Sure." He looked at the werewolf too, who gave them both a clueless shrug.

"How is it safe for me to be here in this house right now? The Black Heron can find us far easier now. Honestly, if I were you, I would've shipped me off in the Winnie and told Romeo to drive me as far away as we could get before those people make another attempt."

"Why's that?" The bearded man's lips twitched beneath his mustache.

"Because...well, I used the coin again. That turns on the tracer thing, right? Which means they can find me? I know it goes away after a few days, but it definitely flared again when I used it. Hence the massive underground battle..." Her gaze darted from one man to the other and she leaned toward them. "Neither of you seem very worried about that."

"We're not." The old man chuckled.

"Um..."

"You kinda turned it off, Lil." Romeo shrugged again but this time, it was in amusement instead of confusion.

"What?"

"I think it was the necklace." He nodded at the mirror charm hanging around her neck—her mom's first magical artifact left as a clue on the trail to find Greta Antony and the Black Heron Society. It was probably the single most powerful item Lily had. *At least the most powerful item that doesn't bring a horde of dark-magic lunatics down on my head.*

"It... Okay, yeah." She raised her hand to finger the mirror charm. "It reverses the most powerful spell just cast, but it didn't undo the blood magic."

"Or your black cloud." Romeo spread his arms. "Maybe it has something to do with not being able to undo the wearer's most powerful spell. I dunno."

"But we think it...erased the tracer brought on by you using that...what do you call it?" Ozias turned toward Romeo.

"The heron coin." He and Lily said it at the same time and smirked at each other.

"Right." The old man stroked his beard a few times. "The brilliant burst of magical energy that would have followed you right now after using the heron coin doesn't actually exist anymore. Because, we assume, the necklace undid it."

"Is that possible?"

The werewolf hesitated, then nodded. "I'm not sure but it makes sense."

"Please tell me you're not simply guessing." She leaned forward over her lap and studied them both. "Tell me that there's actual proof or someone you trust had a way to confirm that it's gone. The last thing I need is to think I'm safe only to find out I should have known better."

"Well, Lil, you seemed convinced that Castor knew what he was talking about the first time—"

She burst out laughing. "Castor?" *He's literally the last person I expected.* "He said the heron coin's tracer went away?"

Ozias responded with a thoughtful hum. "It was more along the lines of that necklace of yours muddying the scent of your trail."

That made her laugh even harder until the tears rolled from the corners of her eyes, and she couldn't do a thing about it. The older witch and the werewolf chuckled at each other, each unsure as to whether or not she had fully healed or had simply lost her mind. Finally, she brought herself under control and wiped her eyes. "Okay. Okay. Yes, I'm totally willing to take whatever Castor said as a good sign. We'll go with it."

"I'm glad you believe the boy." The old man regarded her with a watchful expression. "Many people tend to find him...unnerving."

"That's because he can see everything we can't." Lily raised an eyebrow and fought back more laughter. "And that kid sees so much."

"Yes." After a deep breath, Ozias exhaled slowly through his nose and took a step closer to the bed. "I can't thank you enough for what you've done here. I know you're going to say I shouldn't because you used the heron coin, etcetera, etcetera, but my people and I got a good deal more out of that than merely winning a fight. At least you've reminded me that not everything has to be black and white, especially now. I knew this already, Lily, but... Well, fear does strange things to people, doesn't it?"

"If they let it, yeah."

He took her hand. "I wish you all the best, and I hope you reach your mother in the exact moment you were meant to. Beyond that, I really hope you give those Black Heron mongrels hell."

She couldn't help but laugh at that too. "That's the plan."

"Good. You're always welcome in Otiylo. It's a safe place for everyone, but I especially mean the two of you." The man wrapped his arms around her in a warm, gentle hug, then turned to shake Romeo's hand. No more words passed between them before the leader of the Greek rebel witches took his leave and closed the door behind him.

Romeo came back to the bed and crawled up on it. He sat behind her and twined his arms around her, and she rested her head back against his chest. "So you saw your mom in Libya, huh?"

"Yeah, I think so. That's as far as the network would show me. They took her out into a desert, from what I could see, and then they simply...disappeared. There's a huge illusion ward. I mean really huge. I think that's what's hiding the main Black Heron meeting place. It's also maybe where they're gonna try to cast the Spell That Should Never Be Uttered."

He chuckled. "BHHQ, huh?"

"Easy." She latched her hands on his forearms folded in front of her and hugged them closer to her chest. "I need to discover how to find my mom again when I need to, without that damn coin. We don't need to go through this again. And I honestly don't want to spend the time going through what's left of that bunker trying to find it."

With his lips pressed to the back of her head, Romeo breathed in the smell of her and gave her a quick kiss. "Yeah, that's definitely off the priority list, I think."

"That's fine with me. As long as you can handle me practicing with that black cloud for hours on end while we head off to Libya this time. I feel like there's so much more that it can do. And maybe I can use the raven like my mom did. You know, to look for her."

"I can handle anything you need to do." He leaned forward and left a quick peck on her cheek. "So can you."

"I'm glad we're on the same page." They laughed and sat there for a minute longer. *I'm totally happy to simply sit here and let him hold me for a while.* Her stomach interrupted the moment with a loud, angry-sounding gurgle. *Not a very long while, I guess.* "Okay, so what does an Optatus witch have to do to get some food around here?"

"Hmm...probably merely desire it more than anything else, right?" He laughed when she slapped his forearm playfully. "Hey, that's how an Optatus works, yeah?"

"I'm trying to use these powers for good, Romeo. Not food."

Slowly, he released her and slid off the bed. "That's a perfectly acceptable distinction. The next best thing is me going to get food for both of us, huh?"

"That sounds good. Then, I guess we can head on out."

"To Libya!" Romeo thrust a finger in the air and

marched through the door to hunt down what would be their very late lunch.

Shaking her head, Lily rubbed her scarred shoulder absently and felt the little tingle of it beneath her own fingers. She sighed. "I'm coming, Mom. Whatever you do, don't give up on me yet."

TWENTY-SIX

"Oh, my God." Lily dropped her head against the headrest of the passenger seat and ran her hands along the armrests. "I never thought sitting in this chair and rolling down the road would make me this happy."

"Home, sweet home, right?" Romeo grinned at her and pulled onto E961, this time heading north again—the only direction they could go—to try to find someone else to ferry them across another body of water. Otherwise, they'd have to drive for a very long time.

"And we can open the windows whenever we want." She rolled hers down a few inches, simply to prove her point. "Fresh air and sunshine. Is it weird that it feels like we have more space in the adventuremobile than in that entire compound underground?"

"Not even a little. Really, if you think about it, the whole world is this RV. And the Winnie is the whole world."

"Um..." She pressed her lips together and shot him a playful frown. "How's that?"

"I'm trying to reinvent 'The world is our oyster.' I think it works."

She laughed and closed her eyes. "Sure. The world is our Winnie." They both snorted, and she snatched his phone from the cupholder in the center console. "I can't believe this only has one crack across the screen."

He scowled. "You can't really say, 'only one crack,' Lily. That's still one too many."

"Wow. Look at you."

Romeo chuckled and looked away from the road at his phone in her hand and then her. "What did I do?"

"I would've pegged you as someone who didn't really care about a cracked phone screen if the phone still actually worked."

"Huh." He shrugged. "I guess you still have a few things to learn about me."

"Oh, right. You know, that's good. I definitely wouldn't want this trip with you to get boring or anything."

"Hey..."

Lily turned his phone's lock screen on and punched in the numbers. Five-four-five-nine. *Why does that feel like it means something? Every time I—* She took a sharp breath and stared at the phone, her mind still focused on the passcode numbers and her gaze on the home screen now. It went black again when she pressed the little button on the side. She pulled the lock screen up one more time to make sure. *Five-four-five-nine. L-I-L-Y.* She stared at the little round buttons with the numbers and their groupings of letters and had no idea how to react to the realization.

"Is everything okay?" He glanced at the phone and adjusted his grip on the steering wheel.

"Yeah. We're good." She punched the numbers in again quickly and pulled up his music app. "I know you told me a while ago, but...you've had this same passcode on for your phone for a while, right?"

"Yep. Probably..." He puffed out a sigh. "Probably since I first got a phone, honestly."

She swallowed. "Any particular reason you chose it?"

"I don't think so." He shrugged, tilted his head, and scratched quickly behind his ear. "I think I simply like the numbers. Sometimes they feel...like the right fit for something, you know?"

"Yeah, I guess." *He's lying. Probably. That's his nervous scratch. Has he seriously walked around for at least the last seven years with my name as the passcode to his phone?* She frowned at the open music app on the screen and barely paid attention to the albums, artists, or songs as she scrolled through. Still, she couldn't help the grin that came with the realization. *He definitely had a phone in eighth grade.*

"Okay, judging by your face right now, I'm gonna say you found something really good."

"What?"

"Music, right?"

Lily looked at his profile and his easy smile as he took them farther and farther on her mom's treasure hunt turned rescue mission. *And it's as important to him as it is to me.* "Yeah, I found something. How about..." She stopped scrolling randomly and blurted out the first song she saw. "'Alexander the Great'?"

Romeo snorted. "By Iron Maiden?"

"Uh...yup."

"That's not really... Okay. I didn't expect you to whip that one out."

"Should we go with shuffle?" She tried to sound serious about it but couldn't hold back a little giggle.

"Yeah, shuffle's good. Right now, I think the only mood we need to set is whatever takes us away from Otiylo and closer to Greta."

"We shoulda made a playlist for that one." They both fought more laughter as she selected *Shuffle All* and the Winnie's updated sound system kicked on with the drums and electric of The Proclaimers' "I'm Gonna Be." "All right. Here we go."

He set his hand palm-up on the center console and wiggled his fingers at her. She took it and had to remind herself to relax both her shoulders at the same time. "You know, Lil. I think you're getting quite good as my DJ apprentice."

"Oh, thank you. But watch out, though. When we hit the epic day when the student becomes the master, it's game over."

He grinned, shook his head, and stared out at the highway ahead and whatever destination awaited them. "Note to self. Don't compliment Lily too much."

"Or she'll play good music all over you."

AFTER SUCH A LATE start on the next leg of their seem-
ingly endless road trip—they'd left Otiylo with full bellies a
little after 2:00 p.m—they didn't make it as far as their
usual daily mileage.

"We can keep going a little longer." Even as Lily said
it, Romeo was already taking the exit for Etoliko.

"I'd ask if you heard what the healer told you, Lil, but
you were right there with me. And you repeated it to her."

"Yeah. Take it easy for twenty-four hours." She
glanced at the palm trees that flashed past on the side of
the road. "But that's literally all I've done while you drive.
It doesn't take much heavy lifting to sit in the passenger
seat or to be the honorary DJ. Sorry to burst your bubble."

He snorted. "Sitting for a long time in a seat without
getting up doesn't exactly count as taking it easy. Even a
seat as comfy as that one."

"We could at least drive until the sun goes down—"

"Nope. I'm also hungry."

She laughed. "Five hours on the road, huh?"

"You know it."

What she didn't know was that Ozias and his people
had essentially filled the Winnie's fridge and pantry to
bursting with as much food as they could spare, which was
a considerable amount. When he eased to a stop beside a
gas station and called this their stop for the night, she literally gawped at more food than they'd probably bought over
the entire trip. "Is this..." She snatched up a can of pickled
caper leaves and studied the label. "Oh, my God. It is."

"What's up?" He put his elbow on the counter and

cupped his chin in his hands while he grinned innocently at her.

"We spent five hours yesterday organizing all those cans and bottles and packaged things and..." She turned to the pantry and shook her head in disbelief. "Seriously, did they simply empty all those pallets and stick 'em in here?"

He laughed and stepped past the counter toward her. When he slipped his arms around her waist and hugged her from behind, she lifted the can in her hand to make sure they could both see it. "It looks like all our hard work paid off, huh?"

"Romeo, I did not organize all their food so they'd give it to us afterward."

"But it was really nice of them. And I'm very sure that everything we stacked in that particular room was actually destroyed by flying spells. That was our second underground battle, by the way. On two different continents."

"Yeah, okay." She snorted. "That makes me feel a little better, I guess."

"The trashed food or the underground battle part?"

She slipped out of his arms, lifted the can again, and looked at him over her shoulder. "Maybe both."

"Well that's...okay." He took a pot from the cupboard above the stove and set it on the burner for her. "So, I know I said I was hungry..."

"You sure did."

Romeo stepped up behind her again and caught her hips. Lily froze. "But it's been even longer since we've had a bed in a room by ourselves."

"But I woke up in a bed like six hours ago." She pressed her lips together and tried not to laugh.

His lips tickled her ear, followed by a low, heavy growl. "You know what I mean, Lily."

"Uh-huh. And how does that apply more to 'taking it easy' than sitting up front for a few more hours while we keep driving."

"Trust me. You'll be very relaxed in about ten minutes."

She barked out a laugh. "Only ten?"

"Okay, eight. If you're lucky." She chuckled, and his teeth closed softly over her earlobe. A shudder ran down the side of her neck before he whispered, "And then I'll make dinner."

The can of caper leaves thumped onto the kitchen counter, and she spun to kiss him. A second later, he carried her through the doorway into the bedroom, ready to make sure that she continued to take it easy.

TWENTY-SEVEN

The next morning, Lily was up and out of bed barely after sunrise—the first time she could remember being up before Romeo. She actually enjoyed waking up and seeing him asleep there, curled on his side of the bed. Gently, she kissed his cheek, crawled to the foot of the bed, and snagged a sweater from the wardrobe before she stepped outside and greeted the dawn.

"It's time to see what else you can do, Optatus." Calling herself the ancient name for what she apparently was only made it feel more like her new reality. Which it was, obviously. "No more heron coin and no more Black Heron stalkers. There's gotta be a better way to find you, Mom. Totem to totem, maybe."

This time, instead of standing at the edge of the Black Sea while she summoned black clouds, she found a relatively comfortable place on the ground a few feet from the Winnie's side door and crossed her legs. "So, it's all about what I really desire, huh? Okay. That seems easy enough."

She clapped once and summoned the black cloud, which responded to her command like it did every other time. Something about this particular casting felt different, however. *This is so much easier.* She drew her hands apart and conjured the swirling, dark energy between her palms in a little over half the time it normally took her—even with all the practice she'd put in. Her arms felt strong and nothing trembled. The quickly healed scar tingled a little, but that would probably pass fairly soon.

Don't let any of this distract you, Lily. Focus on what you want.

With her eyes closed, she let herself feel the power that had always been in her blood—in Greta Antony's blood too —and was now between her hands. She pictured the last shadow-raven she'd conjured on the beach in Romania followed by the much larger raven made of smoke and shadow that had appeared always at the last minute to warn her or protect her. Her inner vision focused on the image of the charred-black bird, its wings spread wide, that her mom had left as proof of her capture inside the cage beneath Ichacál. Finally, she recalled the dream of her mom flying across the world, her arms grasped in the talons of the massive black bird that swooped through the skies.

I want to see—

The energy that fueled the black cloud burst out of her in a plume of shadow and smoke, and she opened her eyes in time to see another of her own conjured ravens thrust from her chest. In the next moment, her vision changed completely and she gasped.

She saw what the raven now saw as it rose into the sky,

headed west, and moved faster than she had thought possible. Highways and roads, farms and cities and towers, and stretches of untouched land flitted below her in seconds. The raven continued, propelled by the force of an Optatus' greatest desire in that moment. The young witch didn't recognize anything she saw below her as it slid beneath the raven's shadow. But she would if her mom was still behind that same wall of shimmering orange-brown magic.

"Woah." The Winnie's side door slammed shut behind Romeo and interrupted her spell.

A little grunt of released pressure escaped her, and she doubled over her crossed legs to clear her head and catch her breath. He was on his knees beside her in an instant, pushed her up by the shoulders, and stared at her in concern. "Lily? Hey. Lily, what were you—"

"I think I did it, Romeo." When she looked at him, her grin was wide and triumphant.

He huffed a sigh and sat back on his heels. "You scared the crap out of me, you know that?"

"The raven or me simply sitting here?"

"Uh...maybe both." He smirked but still couldn't hide the worried frown that had darkened his green eyes. "This is definitely not taking it easy, no matter how you wanna spin it."

"My shoulder's fine." She reached out for his hand and he stood before he took hers and helped her up. "I'm fine. And I summoned another raven."

That definitely caught his attention and he studied her face for a few seconds and pursed his lips. "It did something this time, huh?"

"Oh, yeah. I can...see what it sees."

"Seriously?"

She nodded, and a baffled laugh escaped him. "Well, I'm obviously gonna have to practice that too, but it felt so much easier this time. Like I'm...I dunno. Tapping into something, finally."

"Okay." He shrugged, put a hand on her back, and guided her toward the Winnie again. "Let's take a break on the tapping and have breakfast. Then we'll talk about how we're gonna work the rest of it out."

Lily let him lead her to their house on wheels, smiling the whole time. She frowned when a completely different thought intruded. "Am I turning into my mom?"

He laughed and opened the side door for her. "I think in your case, Lil, that's the opposite of a bad thing. Come on." They stepped inside together, and the door shut with another bang.

About a dozen yards away from where the young witch and her werewolf companion had camped their vehicle for the night, the watcher crouched behind a cluster of dry, prickly bushes. He'd followed them since halfway between here and Otiylo when he'd caught scent of something he hadn't smelled in so long, he almost didn't recognize it. But he knew instantly that he'd found another Optatus witch.

"Two on the same road in as many days," he whispered and rubbed his gnarled, green-tinted hands. "They are the ones. I know it."

With a smug grin, the watcher turned from his hiding place and flashed a mouthful of sharp, pointed teeth at the surrounding wilderness. "Royal will love this. Yes. And I'll be the one to tell him." With a last glance at the Winnebago and the dark forms of his newest discovery moving inside, he bounded away from the bushes and snapped his fingers. He vanished into thin air before his large, clawed feet left the ground again on his way to make history.

The End

WHILE LILY and Romeo search for her mother, they are set upon to find an artifact they need to help get to Greta. Find out what lengths the couple are willing to go to find Greta in *Return of the Witch.*

Get sneak peeks, exclusive giveaways, behind the scenes content, and more.

PLUS you'll be notified of special **one day only fan pricing** on new releases.

Sign up today to get free stories.

CLICK HERE

or visit: https://marthacarr.com/read-free-stories/

For Hire: Teachers for special school in Virginia countryside.

Must be able to handle teenagers with special abilities.

Cannot be afraid to discipline werewolves, wizards, elves and other assorted hormonal teens.

Apply at the School of Necessary Magic.

AVAILABLE AT AMAZON RETAILERS

Getting ready to leave for NYC for one of my oldest friend's, David's birthday. He is a native of Manhattan. I'm not sure how many of those there really are. Kind of like Austin, where I live. Most of us are from somewhere else.

I met David when I was thirty years old, a new journalist with a small baby and I was interviewing his mother, Lillian Vernon of the catalogue fame for a business article. David was in charge of her PR. To this day, exactly thirty years later, I remember four things most of all from that interview. That Lillian Vernon said what she wanted to say, no filters. David kept sputtering behind her, and I'd look up at him and back at Lillian waiting for a retraction but nope. Lillian Vernon always spoke her mind and didn't wait to see if you were okay with it. Second thing was she liked genuine people and couldn't put up with phonies.

It didn't matter to her if you had money or not. Were you interested in the world? Did you do what you said you would do? And most important, were you kind to others?

At the time I felt incredibly old. I mean, I was thirty years old after all, and a newly divorced single mother with a small baby starting a new career. My life was over, and I had started everything late. That's also exactly what I told my eighty-year-old godmother at the time, with no irony in my voice.

But I was curious and compassionate and kind of funny even then, and Lillian took to me and I took to her. I started getting invitations to a lot of swanky events and a nice discount from the catalogue. The Offspring's picture even appeared in a lot of picture frames when he was little. Later, when I started writing books Lillian gave me a quote for the back of every book.

Her son, David and I became instant pals despite always living states apart from each other. There were those two years I lived in the city and got to see the 4th of July fireworks from her penthouse, which had a Michelangelo drawing in it that I swear I didn't touch. I was also dating a very cute prosecutor at the time and when David met him, he looked at me and said, "My opinion of you has gone up."

That third and fourth thing I remember to this day were two lines she said that of course I quoted in the article, much to David's chagrin. The first was, "The first thing a woman should do when she gets a job is hire a maid. They won't put on your tombstone, she did it all, she had no help." The second line was, "The best thing the old-line feminists can do for women today is get out of the way." By the way, she was one of those old-line feminists who had broken down a lot of corporate doors.

I remember thinking, some day I want to be this bold, this sure of myself and ask this easily for what I need with an expectation that I'll find it, or it'll find me.

Well, here I am at the age Lillian was when we met and still hanging out with her son. Party over here! Instead of being at the start of a career, I'm in the last hurrah, which could turn out to be another thirty years, of course. There's a lot of articles and columns and books behind me and a lot of hard-won wisdom here in the present. Main thing I've learned? Just make sure you pick what you love to do so that on the days it's not going well, you're still glad you're there. Then, when thirty years have gone by, you can look back and see that it's been a great ride with more adventures to follow.

Thank you for joining us on this adventure!

I love Martha's quote: "Just make sure you pick what you love to do so that on the days it's not going well, you're still glad you're there."

It says something similar to a little "feel good" picture one of my mentors, Spence Nimberger.

Spence had a 5x8 image of a golf course with a quote similar. "Do what you love and you will never work a day in your life."

I was in my twenties when I read that. Old enough to realize there was wisdom there, but yet not wise enough to implement the wisdom it contained.

If I could deliver anything to my three sons and get them to really grasp the nuance, it would be that message. Find what you love, figure out a way to make a living doing it, and be happy. Because even in your worse weeks, it is still better than the best week at a job you hate.

I'm fortunate it only took me fifty years to find my

passion, my avocation. (If you knew me when I was younger, you might be excused for believing a rock had a better chance of becoming wise than I did.)

Now, I work on trains, plains, and automobiles as I travel around the world. I'm working (like right now on a trip between Frankfurt and Paris), but yet it doesn't suck. As many of you know who read my *Author Notes*, traveling isn't a big passion of mine.

But we have a lot of travel required for the business (conferences and book fairs), so I'm on the road a lot. Plus, I need to see new places to give the imagination a reservoir of creativity as I plot new books.

Travel helps accomplish that.

I believe that as I grow into my 60s (another eight years), I'll settle down and not travel as much. There will be others in the company who need to figure out how to keep their eyes open as jetlag lashes their body and their brains try to figure out why there is light in the sky when the body rhythm swears it should be dark.

I really, really hate to feel sleepy, ergo I don't like to deal with jetlag, which means I don't want to travel. BUT —I love the profession I am in, and would not give up the chance to create stories, publish books, and meet fans from around the world because of jetlag.

Great, now that last paragraph has me realize that there is no way I could be a Ranger or anything particularly hard in the military. They would tell me I'd have to stay up seventy-two hours, and I'd be, "Yeah, eject me now, buddy. Mike wants his sleep."

"Bullshit! You stay awake!"

"Yeah, no can dozzzzz…"

(Somewhere above, the message was supposed to be "Do what you love and you won't work (much) in your life." It ended up, "Fuck Ranger school. I need sleep and jetlag sucks.")

On to work on *Witch of the Federation* Book 04.03 ;-)

Michael

Other series:

THE LAST VAMPIRE
THE WITCH NEXT DOOR

OTHER BOOKS BY JUDITH BERENS

OTHER BOOKS BY MARTHA CARR

JOIN THE ORICERAN UNIVERSE FAN GROUP ON FACEBOOK!

CONNECT WITH THE AUTHORS

Martha Carr Social

Website: http://www.marthacarr.com

Facebook: https://www.facebook.com/
groups/MarthaCarrFans/

Michael Anderle Social

Michael Anderle Social
Website:
http://www.lmbpn.com

Email List:
http://lmbpn.com/email/

Facebook Here: https://www.
facebook.com/TheKurtherianGambitBooks/